FROM THE
NANCY DREW FILES

THE CASE: Go undercover at a Texas ranch to find the kidnappers who are demanding a small fortune—for a girl who's been dead for fifteen years.

CONTACT: Robert Reigert, retired oil tycoon, cattle baron, and father of the kidnapped girl.

SUSPECTS: Jonelle, Reigert's flashy new wife. She seems more concerned with his money than his welfare.

Mark Blake, Jonelle's handsome young son. He has big plans for running the ranch—his way.

Senora Arguello, Reigert's trusted housekeeper. She's been caught going through his personal effects.

Joe Bob, the ranch hand and rodeo clown who seems to be around every time Nancy has an "accident."

COMPLICATIONS: Nancy is on her own, undercover, and forty miles from the nearest town. She can't afford to trust anyone, including Gene Newsom, handsome foreman of the ranch. The only thing she can depend on is trouble—western style.

Books in THE NANCY DREW FILES® Series

#1 SECRETS CAN KILL
#2 DEADLY INTENT
#3 MURDER ON ICE
#4 SMILE AND SAY MURDER
#5 HIT AND RUN HOLIDAY
#6 WHITE WATER TERROR
#7 DEADLY DOUBLES
#8 TWO POINTS TO MURDER
#9 FALSE MOVES
#10 BURIED SECRETS
#11 HEART OF DANGER
#12 FATAL RANSOM
#13 WINGS OF FEAR
#14 THIS SIDE OF EVIL
#15 TRIAL BY FIRE
#16 NEVER SAY DIE
#17 STAY TUNED FOR DANGER

#18 CIRCLE OF EVIL
#19 SISTERS IN CRIME
#20 VERY DEADLY YOURS
#21 RECIPE FOR MURDER
#22 FATAL ATTRACTION
#23 SINISTER PARADISE
#24 TILL DEATH DO US PART
#25 RICH AND DANGEROUS
#26 PLAYING WITH FIRE
#27 MOST LIKELY TO DIE
#28 THE BLACK WIDOW
#29 PURE POISON
#30 DEATH BY DESIGN
#31 TROUBLE IN TAHITI
#32 HIGH MARKS FOR MALICE
#33 DANGER IN DISGUISE

Available from ARCHWAY paperbacks

THE NANCY DREW FILES CASE · 11

HEART OF DANGER

Carolyn Keene

AN ARCHWAY PAPERBACK
Published by POCKET BOOKS
New York   London   Toronto   Sydney   Tokyo

AN ARCHWAY PAPERBACK *Original*

An Archway Paperback published by
POCKET BOOKS, a division of Simon & Schuster Inc.
1230 Avenue of the Americas, New York, NY 10020

ISBN: 0-671-68728-X

First Archway Paperback printing May 1987

10 9 8 7 6 5 4 3 2

Chapter

One

I WISH YOU didn't have to go." Ned Nickerson's lips brushed Nancy Drew's cheek as he held her tightly in his arms.

Nancy looked up into his dark eyes. "I do too," she whispered, burying her face against his shoulder. "Texas seems light-years away."

"I wish this Reigert guy had never contacted you," Ned said.

"Oh, Ned, you know the Reigert case is important to me." But as important as the case was, Nancy didn't want to leave Ned. Not when they had just gotten back together again.

Right at that moment Nancy didn't feel like a

detective going off to solve a difficult case; she felt only like a girl saying goodbye to the boy she loved.

She kissed him again. Above them someplace, the airport's public address system announced Nancy's flight for the third time.

Nancy tried to pull away, but Ned's arms tightened around her. "Listen, if you need help," he said, "I could come down for a long weekend or even take a couple of days off from school. Also, my uncle Al lives in Dallas, and by plane he's not too far from where you'll be. He'd come running to help you—I know he would. He's a great guy—works for one of the Dallas newspapers."

"Thanks for the offer," Nancy said with a smile. "I'll take you up on it if things get really tough."

Reluctantly Nancy drew away from Ned. "I'm going," she said, slinging her carry-on bag over her shoulder and picking up her portable typewriter. She smoothed her skirt and adjusted her trim khaki blazer. "Well, do I look ready?"

"You look perfect," Ned said, giving her a final, quick kiss. "Hey, Nancy Drew," he said in a husky voice, "don't forget that I love you."

Once on the plane Nancy flipped open her notebook to review the notes she had made during her telephone call with Robert Reigert a few days earlier. Mr. Reigert, at sixty-five, was a retired Texas oil tycoon. He had read a newspaper article about Nancy's having solved an old mystery and been impressed enough to call her when he needed a detective to solve the case of his two-year-old daughter's disappearance fifteen years earlier.

He told her she would have to work undercover and alone at his ranch, Casa del Alamo. The ranch was a hundred miles west of San Antonio and forty miles from the nearest town. Forty miles from help, if I need it, thought Nancy.

She looked down at her notes again. If there had been any clues to the girl's disappearance, they were long gone, lost in the mountains of Mexico, in the debris of the private plane crash that killed Mr. Reigert's wife, Isabel. Mother and daughter had been on their way to visit Isabel's wealthy, aristocratic Mexican family. The woman's body had been found at the site of the crash, but the girl had simply disappeared.

For years Mr. Reigert had believed that his daughter wandered away from the crash and died alone in the mountains. But just before his call to Nancy, he received a hand-printed ransom note saying that Catarina, now seventeen, was still alive and being held! Attached to the note, which had been slipped under his front door, was a faded scrap of cloth that Mr. Reigert insisted was a piece of the dress Catarina had been wearing when she left.

Nancy looked at her notebook again. A ransom

note and a fifteen-year-old scrap of cloth that might or might not be what Mr. Reigert thought it was. Precious little to go on.

But the story of Catarina had touched Nancy because she, too, had lost her mother years before. She wondered what would have happened if she had lost her father as well and been brought up by strangers? She definitely had a deep personal interest in Catarina Reigert and felt compelled to accept the case.

Anyway, she told herself, snapping her notebook shut, the trail wasn't so cold as it seemed. That ransom note, for instance, hadn't been written fifteen years before. It had to have come from someone who had easy access to the Reigert house—maybe even someone who worked at the ranch. That was what Mr. Reigert seemed to think. Her first task, she knew, would be to get acquainted with everyone at Casa del Alamo.

Nancy looked down at the portable typewriter she had stowed under her seat. For this job, she wouldn't be Nancy Drew, Girl Detective. She was going as Nancy Driscoll, a ghostwriter sent to help Mr. Reigert write his memoirs. It was a good cover because she could ask questions and snoop around the ranch without appearing suspicious. She had brought the typewriter, a camera, and several notebooks to help with her disguise. She was all set.

* * *

"So, you're a writer, huh?" Mark Blake asked with a smile as he picked up Nancy's luggage and started out to the parking lot of the San Antonio airport.

"Yes," Nancy said, studying her companion covertly. Mr. Reigert had sent his twenty-five-year-old stepson, Mark, to pick Nancy up and drive her to the ranch. Mark was tall, dark, and good-looking, but his charming smile had an arrogant twist to it. Nancy wasn't sure she liked it or him. He was wearing a fancy cowboy shirt, with jeans and snakeskin boots.

"It's funny the old man didn't tell my mother and me about working on his memoirs," Mark observed, tossing Nancy's bag into the backseat of a white Cadillac.

"Perhaps it was a sudden inspiration," Nancy remarked noncommittally. She looked at the car. Mark Blake certainly drove an expensive automobile. "Your mother must be the second Mrs. Reigert," she added. "I understand that Mr. Reigert's first wife died in a plane crash."

"That's right," Mark said, climbing into the car. "But that was a long time ago. He and Jonelle got married last year."

"Jonelle?"

"My mother," Mark said. "I call her that sometimes."

"Oh," Nancy murmured. "How did she and Mr. Reigert meet?"

"It's a long story," Mark said, starting the car. He gave her another charming smile that made deep dimples in his cheeks. "Why do you want to know?"

Nancy smiled back. "Part of my job," she replied, pushing back her red-gold hair. "If I'm going to help Mr. Reigert, I need to know about his family."

"Yeah, I suppose." Mark shrugged. "Anyway, it's no big secret. They met at a club in Dallas, where Jonelle was a hostess." He laughed. "You might call it a whirlwind romance. In a couple of weeks they were married and we were living at the ranch."

"Do you work at the ranch?" Nancy asked, looking at Mark's boots.

"Me? You mean, punching cattle? Heck, no. I'm into investments." Mark quickly turned his head to glance at Nancy. "You know, you don't quite fit my image of a ghostwriter."

Nancy grinned back. "Well, I guess ghostwriters come in all shapes and sizes."

"Yes, but you look so young," Mark persisted.

"I got an early start." Nancy realized that she should have thought more about her cover. "My—my father helped me in the beginning."

Before Mark could ask any other questions, she started asking some of her own. Mark's answers were all friendly enough. But she got the feeling that his easy charm wasn't quite sincere.

It was late afternoon and the sun was dipping

toward the horizon. As they drove toward the west, the hills became steeper and rockier, and the vegetation more sparse and brown. Low, gnarled mesquite trees were interspersed with clumps of dark green cedars and gray green sage. Spiky clumps of prickly pear cactus grew among the grasses. Grazing in a stand of oak trees, Nancy counted five small deer, all brown with white markings on their tails.

"White-tailed deer," Mark told Nancy. "The only native deer in this country. They're small, but around here hunting is very big business and the size of the deer doesn't matter."

They turned off the main road and drove under an impressive stone archway that bore the words Casa del Alamo and what looked like a ranch brand, a circle with an *R* in it.

Finally, at the end of the two- or three-mile-long lane, they came to a low, sprawling house with a red tile roof, shaded by several huge old cottonwood trees. The house had a wide, Spanish-style veranda across the front, and heavy shutters stood open at all the windows. It was all surrounded by a luxuriant green lawn and a colorful garden. As they pulled up to the main entrance, a woman stepped onto the veranda.

"You must be Nancy Driscoll," she said as Nancy got out of the car. "I'm Jonelle Reigert." Mrs. Reigert was dressed in designer dude-ranch clothes—tight white pants and a silk shirt with silver buttons. Nancy noticed that the buttons

7

were embossed with the brand she'd seen on the gate.

"I'm glad to meet you, Mrs. Reigert," Nancy said, joining her on the veranda and extending her hand. While her son was dark, Mrs. Reigert was a platinum blonde. She had fixed her hair in an enormous bouffant style. Her carefully made-up mouth wore a vivacious smile, but Nancy thought that it was plastered on and that Jonelle Reigert seemed rather nervous.

"Glad to have you here," Mrs. Reigert said. "We hope you'll enjoy your stay. Mrs. Arguello will show you to your room."

Nancy turned. An elderly Mexican woman stepped silently out of the house. Her high-cheekboned face was like weathered parchment, brown and wrinkled. And her hawklike black eyes were fixed on Nancy, seeming to pierce right through her. She must be seventy years old, perhaps more, Nancy thought. Had she been with Mr. Reigert long enough to know anything about Catarina?

"Follow me, senorita," the old woman said. Mark had set Nancy's bags on the porch, and Nancy bent to pick them up. "No," Mrs. Arguello said simply. She went to the edge of the porch and raised her voice commandingly. "Joe Bob! Pronto!"

A stooped man wearing a shapeless brown jacket of some indefinable leather—perhaps deerskin—appeared from around the corner.

Nancy had the distinct impression that he had been listening there.

Mrs. Reigert smiled again. "This is another member of our staff," she said. "His name is Joe Bob and he looks after the horses."

As Joe Bob picked up Nancy's bags, he glanced furtively at her out of the corner of his eye and muttered something that Nancy couldn't make out. Nancy just about walked into the next person to come out of the house, a tall, good-looking young man, holding a well-worn cowboy hat at his side. His jeans were dusty and faded at the knees, and he wore a blue chambray work shirt.

"Howdy," he said in a broad Texas drawl. "I'll bet you're that writer Mr. Reigert's brought in."

Nancy suppressed a smile. This authentic-looking cowboy made Mark Blake look like a fancy-dress dude. "You're right," she said. "I'm Nancy Driscoll."

"This is Gene Newsom," Mrs. Reigert said. She smiled warmly at Gene and laid a hand on his arm. "Gene is our foreman. We couldn't get along without him—could we, Gene?" Nancy noticed that her voice had taken on a soft, almost purring sound that instantly made Gene uncomfortable. His smile faded and he took a step back, jamming his battered Stetson on his head.

"Good to meet you, Nancy," he said briefly. Then, stepping off the veranda, he was gone quickly.

"Don't let Gene fool you with that cowboy

look," Mrs. Reigert said. "He graduated from Texas A and M at the top of his class. He knows all there is to know about cattle. My husband relies heavily on his ideas about range management."

"That's your trouble, Jonelle," Mark said with thinly disguised contempt. "You're too easily impressed. Just because—"

"Mark," Mrs. Reigert said with a quick glance in Nancy's direction. "Not now." She turned to Joe Bob. "Joe Bob, take those bags to Miss Driscoll's room." Reluctantly, Nancy followed him and Mrs. Arguello. She wished Mrs. Reigert hadn't stopped Mark. She was curious about his animosity toward Gene.

The outside of Mr. Reigert's home looked like a typical southwestern ranch house. But the inside was decorated like a mansion. Each public room was elegantly furnished with Persian rugs covering glossy hardwood floors. There were cabinets filled with silver and crystal, and paintings covered the walls. It looked to Nancy as if the Reigerts had an unlimited decorating budget.

Nancy's bedroom, in a first-floor wing with the other bedrooms, was small but comfortable and beautifully done. There was even a desk for her typewriter and a telephone on the table beside the bed. Nancy pointed to it as Joe Bob put the bags down and left the room.

"Can I use this to make a long-distance call?" she asked Mrs. Arguello. She was thinking of her promise to Ned.

Mrs. Arguello nodded. "If someone is on this line, there is another phone in Senor Reigert's office," she said. "It is a separate line, for the senor to do business."

Nancy turned. "Have you been with Mr. Reigert for a long time?" she asked.

"*Sí.* Since the old days."

"The old days? When the first Mrs. Reigert lived here?"

The woman gave her a wary glance. "*Sí.*"

"Then you must remember their child, Catarina."

Mrs. Arguello refused to meet her eyes. "Perhaps." She shrugged. "Why do you ask?"

At that moment a girl rapped once on the door frame and walked into the room. She was very pretty, close to Nancy's age, with long dark hair and flashing black eyes. She wore a full skirt and a white embroidered peasant blouse and carried herself almost regally.

"Senorita Driscoll?" she asked softly with a heavy Spanish accent.

Mrs. Arguello scowled at the girl. "I thought I told you to stay in the kitchen, Angela," she scolded.

The girl glanced at Nancy and then lowered her eyes. "From Senor Reigert," she said, handing Nancy a white envelope. "A note for Senorita Driscoll."

"Well, let's leave the senorita alone to read it," the old woman said, shepherding Angela to the door. It was almost as if, Nancy thought, Mrs. Arguello didn't want the two of them to meet.

Nancy opened the sealed envelope and took out a folded piece of paper. The writing on it was scrawled in pencil, in a strong slanted hand. "Come to my office at once," she read. "I've received another ransom note!"

Chapter

Two

HERE. READ THIS," Mr. Reigert commanded, thrusting a printed note at Nancy. "I found it here, on my desk, just a few minutes ago." He was sitting at the desk in his office, a large, comfortable room. He wore his white hair long, falling just below his collar. His white beard was neatly clipped. His face was lined, but his blue eyes were still bright and alert, and his voice was strong. Robert Reigert appeared to be a man of great strength and endurance.

"'Still not convinced?'" Nancy read aloud. "'How's this for proof? Get ready for the pay-off.'" She folded up the note. "I'd like to keep this, if you don't mind."

"Keep this too," Mr. Reigert said. "Seeing it once is enough for me." He handed Nancy a tiny shoe with a little silver bell tied to one lace.

"Catarina's?" Nancy asked, turning it over in her hand.

Mr. Reigert nodded. "I bought that pair of shoes for her when I bought the dress. She wore the outfit often. She was wearing it when she left." He smiled a little. "Some things you never forget."

"So you believe that this *is* an authentic note," Nancy said, pulling up a straight chair beside the desk. "You do believe your daughter is alive and being held for ransom."

Mr. Reigert seemed to stare right through her. He shook his head and focused his eyes before answering. "I don't know," he said testily. "If Catarina's alive, where's she been all these years?" He looked out the window and his voice sounded far away. "But if she's alive, she's my only child. My only heir."

Nancy raised her eyebrows. "What about your wife? And your stepson?"

"My stepson?" Mr. Reigert repeated sarcastically and turned back to face Nancy. "The only thing he deserves is to be booted right off this ranch—him and his harebrained ideas. As for his mother . . . well, she's the worst mistake I ever made in my life." He gave a short laugh. "Except for the time I bought those three dry holes out in the Pecos. Put down a mile of pipe and got nothing

14

but sand and salt water. Cost me a blasted fortune and didn't yield a cent."

Nancy waited a moment. When Mr. Reigert didn't say anything else, she asked, "Tell me about Isabel. She was Mexican?"

"Yes, an aristocrat. Traced herself back to some Spanish ancestor, proud as could be. And beautiful too." A look of pain crossed his face. "Beautiful and spirited, like some wild horse. Couldn't be saddle broken, either by love or by will. We got into a fuss, and she decided she was going back to Mexico, along with our daughter. That's when the plane crashed, as I told you."

"And there's been no word of the girl all these years?" Nancy asked.

"It's like my daughter was swallowed up by the mountains," Mr. Reigert said. He shook his head. "Catarina's the one who should get this ranch—or whatever I can keep safe for her from those two vultures out there. That's why I've sent for you. To find her—if she's still alive." He looked at Nancy. "Have you met Gene?"

"Your foreman? Yes, I met him when I arrived."

"Good. He's the only one around here I trust anymore. Can't even trust Mrs. Arguello now— caught her snooping a couple months ago. Would've fired her if she hadn't been here so long. But Gene's different—honest as the day is long. I want him to show you the ranch. You can't understand my affairs until you see the land. Tell

15

Gene to saddle you up a horse and take you out first thing tomorrow."

"But I think I'd better—" Nancy began. She was about to say that she thought she ought to spend the morning talking with the others, but Mr. Reigert interrupted her.

"Don't care what you think, young lady," he growled. He picked up some papers. "Now get out of here and get on with your detecting."

Nancy went back to her room, where she found a plate of cold sandwiches and a glass of iced tea. Mr. Reigert was certainly an unpleasant and demanding client, she thought as she sat down to eat. She sighed, feeling very much alone. She wished that Ned were there, so she could discuss the situation with him. The next day she would give him a call.

Breakfast at the ranch was a community affair, with everyone sitting down to a table piled with Mrs. Arguello's wonderful Mexican food—tortillas filled with sausage and cheese and red-hot *huevos rancheros*. Nancy went to breakfast wearing jeans, a red and white plaid shirt, a tooled leather belt, and her cowboy boots. Mr. Reigert was not at the table.

Gene glanced at her approvingly. "Looks like you're ready for your tour of the ranch," he said.

Mark set his empty coffee cup down with a bang. "A tour?" he asked suspiciously. "Why?"

"Because your stepfather suggested it," Nancy

said. "He thought I ought to get acquainted with the ranch."

Mrs. Reigert put her hand on her son's arm and smiled at Nancy. "Did you see Mr. Reigert last night?" she asked smoothly. She was wearing a red silk shirt with white fringe.

"For a few minutes," Nancy said. "I hope to talk to him again today, so we can start our work."

"I'm not sure that will be possible," Mrs. Reigert said. "He was very ill this morning."

"Ill?" Nancy asked sharply. Mr. Reigert hadn't shown any signs of illness yesterday evening.

Mrs. Reigert gave a distressed sigh and reached for another tortilla. "He seems to have a chronic stomach problem," she said. "I've been trying to persuade him to see a doctor for the last two or three months, but he refuses. He's so stubborn."

"He's crazy," Mark said, leaning across the table to help himself to the tortillas. "If he'd listen to reason about the stock or anything, he'd—"

Mrs. Arguello had appeared behind Mark with a pot of steaming coffee. As he sat back the two of them collided, and hot coffee splashed onto his arm.

"Ow!" he screeched. "Look what you've done!" Mrs. Arguello stood silently behind him. Nancy thought she saw an inscrutable smile playing at the corners of the old woman's mouth. "I keep telling you, Jonelle," he snarled, "you ought to get rid of this old woman. She's nothing but trouble!"

17

"Now, Mark," Mrs. Reigert said. "Mrs. Arguello didn't mean—"

"Shall we get going?" Gene said to Nancy, pointedly ignoring Mark and his mother. He pushed his chair back and stood up, his face set. "It gets pretty hot out there by noon."

In the corral Joe Bob had saddled up two horses, a gentle palomino for Nancy and a big bay for Gene. Her notebook in her back pocket, Nancy climbed into the saddle and they started off across a grassy pasture. They rode in silence for a few minutes while Nancy absorbed the early-morning beauty. The sky was crystalline and cloudless, and the breeze was flavored with tangy sage.

"What does Mark Reigert have against Mrs. Arguello?" Nancy asked suddenly.

Gene shrugged and lifted his reins. His horse broke into a smooth canter. "Mrs. Arguello's been around for close to twenty years," he said. "She's a fixture. I don't think she takes to newcomers. She's protective of the old man."

"Maybe she thinks he shouldn't have married the second Mrs. Reigert," Nancy prodded.

"Oh, I wouldn't say that," Gene replied quickly.

Nancy changed the line of her questioning. "What about the girl, Angela?" she asked. "Is she a newcomer too?"

Gene turned around in his saddle. "Yeah," he said with a scowl. "She came a few months ago. Why are you asking? *She* certainly can't have anything to do with Mr. Reigert's memoirs. She's just a housemaid."

Nancy looked at Gene, surprised at what sounded like defensiveness. But she didn't have time to think about it, for he reined up and pointed across the pasture toward a herd of black cattle with big humps on their backs.

"Brangus," he said abruptly, changing the subject. "The main breed on the ranch. They're a mixture of Black Angus and Brahma cattle. They stand the heat well and they're good producers."

"What happened to Texas longhorns?" Nancy asked. "They seem to belong with land like this."

"Oh, there're a few of those around here too," Gene replied. "But their meat production isn't that great." He grinned. "These days we go for a little more meat and a little less personality."

Nancy looped the reins around the saddle horn and pulled out her notebook. If she was supposed to be a writer, she decided, she had better take a few notes. "What did Mark mean," she asked idly, still writing, "when he said that Mr. Reigert wouldn't listen to reason about the stock?"

Gene grinned. "Last year Mark had this crazy idea that we ought to get out of the cattle business and into exotic game. It wasn't a very popular idea around the ranch."

"Exotic game?"

"Yeah. A few ranchers are stocking buffalo and exotic breeds of wild sheep. Mark thinks we could make a fortune selling hunting leases, but Mr. Reigert won't hear of it."

"Is Mark right? Why wouldn't Mr. Reigert listen to him?"

Gene shrugged. "Mark could be right, actually. But Mr. Reigert pointed out that we'd need a lot of money to get started. We'd have to enclose the whole place with a six-foot fence, for starters. And the truth is, there isn't much extra money these days. The oil industry isn't doing well, and the cattle market's just as bad."

For the next hour Gene talked about Casa del Alamo's ranching operation, the herds of fat cattle grazing in the grasslands, and the occasional wild-life they saw. The terrain grew rougher as they continued their ride. An irregular-shaped bluff rose to the west, mounded with broken rock and dense underbrush. A V-shaped valley opened out ahead of them, filled with willows and mesquite.

"Oh, look!" Nancy pointed excitedly as a large brown deer darted away through the trees. "Did you see that funny-looking deer? He had spots and big antlers!"

"A buck with spots?" Gene laughed, reining his horse in. "Around here, only fawns have spots, and they sure don't have antlers. Your writer's imagination is working overtime, Nancy."

"But I *saw* him," Nancy protested. "He was

brown, with big white splotches all over him. And he was big, about the size of an elk."

"And he also had a horn in the middle of his forehead, maybe, like the mythical unicorn?" Gene said, teasing her. He added, "The only deer around here are white-tailed deer. The fawns lose their spots after the first season, and even the biggest bucks aren't any bigger than a small calf— certainly not the size of an elk." He turned his horse. "Come on. I think the sun's getting to you. We'd better go back to the house."

I know what I saw, Nancy thought stubbornly as they turned around. But it didn't seem important enough to argue about, or even to give much thought to. More important were the other questions that continually played through her mind like a stuck record. Was Catarina Reigert still alive, held somewhere nearby by kidnappers? Who had delivered the ransom notes?

Nancy didn't have enough clues even to begin to answer the questions. And, while the morning's ride had been pleasant enough, it hadn't taken her an inch further toward solving the mystery.

Nancy and Gene rode into the corral and dismounted. Joe Bob and the other cowboys were nowhere to be seen.

"Now where's he gone off to?" Gene muttered, uncinching the saddle from Nancy's palomino. He handed Nancy a currycomb. "Since Joe Bob isn't around, we'll have to do this job ourselves," he said. "Give her a good rubdown, and then we'll turn her into the stable with a bucket of oats and—"

"Gene!" called a voice.

Nancy turned around. It was Mrs. Reigert, running toward them, her hair flying in the breeze.

"Gene!" she gasped. "You've got to come quickly, before it's too late!"

"What's wrong?" he asked. "What's happened?"

"It's Robert," she cried. "He's very sick. I'm afraid he's dying!"

Chapter
Three

Mrs. Reigert, nearly incoherent, couldn't give them any details of her husband's illness. While Gene helped her into the house, Nancy raced for Mr. Reigert's bedroom, which was down the hall from her own. In the hallway she met Mrs. Arguello, standing guard at his door.

"How is he?" Nancy asked breathlessly.

Mrs. Arguello looked down her nose at Nancy, her black eyes unreadable. "He is sick," she said.

"Is he dying?" Nancy asked, trying to peer in through the partly open door. "What does the doctor say?"

"Doctor? Are you kidding?" Mark asked. "He won't let anyone call a doctor."

23

Nancy turned. Mark was lounging against the wall, a little farther down the hall. "But if he's dying," she insisted, "you ought to call one anyway. It doesn't matter what he says."

"What gave you the idea that I'm dying?" a querulous voice called from the bedroom. "I've just got a bad stomachache, that's all."

Mark grinned as Mrs. Arguello hurried back into the room. "What did I tell you?" he asked.

"But your mother—"

"Jonelle's inclined to dramatize things when she gets a little panicky," Mark interrupted.

"Senorita Driscoll, Senor Reigert wishes to see you," Mrs. Arguello said, coming out of the door. She glanced at Mark. "Alone," she added. Mark glared at her and left.

The room was dark. "Open the shutters," a voice commanded weakly.

Nancy obeyed. In the bright sunlight Nancy could see that the room, unlike the rest of the house, was sparsely furnished—a bed, a chair, a dresser. The only wall decorations were a pair of spurs and a coiled lasso hanging beside the casement window that opened onto the garden. And the only concessions to the electronic age were a TV set on a stand in a corner and a VCR beneath it. The streaming light revealed Mr. Reigert stretched out on the bed. Nancy went to his side.

"How are you feeling?" she asked.

"I'm sick," Mr. Reigert said petulantly. His tanned face looked pale. "Any fool can see that."

"Then why won't you call a doctor?"

"Can't trust doctors, especially that young whippersnapper over in Rio Hondo. I'll get better. Always do." He glared at her fiercely. "What have you found out so far about my daughter?"

"Mr. Reigert," Nancy said, "I followed your instructions this morning—I took a tour of the ranch. Anyway, you've got to be realistic. Finding out the truth about your daughter is certainly not something I can accomplish overnight."

Mr. Reigert frowned at her. "Nonsense," he said. "I've looked into your background. You've got a reputation for accomplishing the impossible —if not overnight, then certainly over the next week." He turned his face away. "So get on with it. I expect to see results."

Getting on with it, Nancy was discovering, wasn't exactly easy. Pad and pencil in hand, as though she were a writer on assignment, Nancy went in search of Mrs. Reigert after lunch. She found her in her room, reclining on a chaise longue with a damp cloth across her forehead. She was dressed in a pink satin robe, trimmed with ivory-colored lace.

"I'm sorry, my dear," Mrs. Reigert said, opening her eyes weakly. "I—I guess I panicked. But I truly thought that Robert was dying. I just hope I didn't make *too* much of a fool of myself."

"Of course you didn't," Nancy said consolingly. She looked around. Mrs. Reigert's room was very different from her husband's. The walls were pale mauve and the floor was thickly carpeted in white. Lacy white curtains hung at the open casement windows. Everything else was pink, with lavish touches of silver and crystal. The dressing table was crowded with makeup and perfume, and the open closet door revealed racks of expensive dresses and dude-ranch clothes.

Nancy turned back to Mrs. Reigert. "Anyone would be concerned in a situation like that, I'm sure," she said. "Mr. Reigert has had these attacks before?"

"Oh, yes. Poor dear, he seems to get better right away, but every time he's a little weaker. Of course"—Mrs. Reigert sighed—"it's his age."

"Of course," Nancy said, smiling a little at the idea of anyone calling the crusty Mr. Reigert "poor dear." She opened her notebook. The best way to get to Mrs. Reigert, she had decided, was through flattery. "My job here," she went on, "is to help your husband with his memoirs. You're *such* an important part of the story that I thought I'd start with you first."

Mrs. Reigert pulled the cloth down over her eyes, obviously uncomfortable with Nancy's inquiry. "Oh, there isn't very much to tell," she said. "I grew up in Dallas. That's where I—I married Mark's father."

"And your name before you married Mr. Reigert?" Nancy asked, jotting rapidly.

"Why does that matter?" she asked.

"It's just for the record," Nancy said reassuringly.

Mrs. Reigert hesitated. "It was—Blake. My name was Jonelle Blake."

"And you were working as a hostess at a club Mr. Reigert used to visit?" Nancy prodded.

"Yes. The Plaza Balcones. It's a dinner club that caters to the very best clientele. That's where I met Robert." She pulled the cloth up on her forehead again and smiled. "He was very attracted to me, and I thought he was just the *sweetest* man."

Nancy had the feeling that learning about Mrs. Reigert's background needed in-depth research. But although it might be interesting to know what Jonelle Blake was doing before she became Jonelle Reigert, Nancy couldn't see that that would have any bearing on the case. Instead, she asked, "What about your son, Mark? What does he do?"

"Oh, he's very interested in ranching, of course."

"But he told me he was more interested in investments," Nancy said, making hasty notes.

Mrs. Reigert looked slightly alarmed. "Well, yes, I suppose he is," she said. "He's always dealing with brokers."

"Actually," Nancy said, glancing down at her notebook, "I'm more interested just now in learning about Mr. Reigert's first family. I'd appreciate it if you could tell me what you know about them."

Mrs. Reigert shifted uneasily. "His first family? How would *I* know anything about his first family?"

"I thought he might have told you—"

"He hasn't told me *anything,*" Mrs. Reigert said flatly. "All I know is that his first wife was killed in a plane crash." She shuddered. "I didn't want to know any more."

"Just the woman? I thought that both his wife and his daughter were killed, even though the girl's body was never found."

Mrs. Reigert shut her eyes and pulled the cloth back down over them. Nancy noticed that her face was *really* pale. "I don't know anything about it," she said in a weak voice. "And now I'm afraid that your other questions will have to wait, my dear. I just don't feel up to answering them right now."

Nancy closed her notebook and stood up. It appeared that there were some things that Mrs. Reigert either didn't know or wouldn't talk about.

Nancy got even less information from Mark than she had from his mother. She found him going through a file drawer in the room he used as an office. He looked up when she came in, and even though he managed a smile, Nancy had the distinct impression that he wasn't happy to see her. He stuffed a folder back into the file and shut it quickly.

"How was your tour of the ranch?" he asked, going to the desk and sitting down.

"Uneventful," Nancy said. She gave him a warm smile. "I understand that you have some rather interesting ideas about the way the ranch ought to be managed."

"Yes, actually, I do," Mark said. He twisted the silver bracelet he was wearing. "But the old man doesn't listen to me. He only listens to Gene."

"Really?"

"Yes, really. He's got a potential gold mine here, and he's ignoring it."

"You mean, turning this place into an exotic game ranch?"

"How'd you find out about that?" Mark demanded.

"Gene told me," Nancy said. "By the way," she added curiously, "I saw something interesting this morning—a big deer, big as an elk, with white spots. Gene says there's no such animal."

To Nancy's surprise, Mark went rigid. "You saw what?" he asked. And then, recovering somewhat, he said, "You're crazy. There's no such thing. The only deer around here are whitetails. And white-tailed fawns may have spots, but they sure don't have antlers."

"But I *saw* it," Nancy insisted. "It ran through the mesquite trees right beside the trail."

"You mean, you *thought* you saw it," Mark said. He stood up, his eyes intent on hers. "For once, Gene's absolutely right. There's no such animal." He picked up a sheaf of papers and reached for the telephone on the desk. "Now, if you'll excuse me, I've got some telephoning to do. My broker is waiting for me to call."

After dinner that evening, Nancy went to her room to make her own phone call—to Ned. It was something she'd been looking forward to all day, and the familiar sound of Ned's voice warmed her.

"How's it going out there?" he asked after he'd been called to the phone by his fraternity brother. "Have you found anything?"

"Just a minute," Nancy said. She put down the phone and got up to make sure the door was securely closed. She didn't want anybody to overhear. "Not much," she said in a low voice when she got back to the phone. "There's been another note, with a shoe that Mr. Reigert says was his daughter's." She told him the details and then added, "I intended to talk to him at length today, but he was sick."

"Sick?"

"Yes. Apparently some chronic stomach ailment. It doesn't seem too serious." She rubbed her back, smiling ruefully. "Speaking of ailments, I sure could use a back rub. I spent the morning on horseback looking at cows, and I'm really stiff."

Ned chuckled. "I thought you were there to look for a lost girl, not lost cows."

"Actually," Nancy said, "it wasn't a cow that intrigued me. It was a deer. A spotted deer with antlers. But I'm being accused of having an overactive imagination. Apparently, such a thing doesn't exist down here."

"A spotted deer?" Ned asked curiously. "I can ask my uncle in Dallas. He's a hunter. If anybody would know, he would." There was a silence. "Hey, you know something, Nancy Drew?" Ned asked, in a softer voice. "I miss you."

"I miss you too," Nancy said, her pulse racing at the tender sound of his voice. "I wish . . ." Her voice trailed away, and she closed her eyes, thinking of the way his lips had felt on hers when they said goodbye at the airport.

"Yeah?" Ned prompted, amused. "What do you wish?"

"I wish you were here," Nancy said. She laughed a little. "I sound like a postcard. 'Having a wonderful time. Wish you were here.'"

"Mmm," Ned said. "Don't tempt me, Nan. I just might get on the next plane and—"

At that moment, there was a soft knock on Nancy's door. "Listen, Ned, I've got to say goodbye. Somebody's at the door."

"Okay. Be careful—and call tomorrow."

"I will," she promised and hung up, hurrying to the door. A folded piece of white paper had been slid underneath it. Nancy picked it up. "Come to the stables immediately," the note said. It was hand lettered. "You'll get all the answers you need." She studied the lettering. She would have to compare it to the notes Mr. Reigert had received, of course, but it didn't look as if it had been written by the same person.

Hurriedly, Nancy found her tiny flashlight and opened her door, looking in both directions. She knew that whoever had slid the note under her door had already disappeared. She crept silently down the shadowy hall and out into the dark yard. The stables were fifty yards away, beyond the corral, and Nancy hurried, her light making a tiny circle of brightness at her feet. Who had put the note under her door? The answer could be an important lead in the case.

The stable door was a darker shadow against the blackness of the wall. Nancy approached it cautiously and went inside, turning off her light. Unfortunately, she kicked a tool leaning against a stall, and it fell over with a clank that echoed in the darkness. Nancy paused, waiting to see what would happen.

Her wait was short. Something solid struck against the side of her head, and she slid into blackness.

Chapter

Four

Nancy opened her eyes. The blackness was replaced by the grayer shadows of the stable. She touched the side of her head. A large bump had already formed, and her head ached miserably.

She felt something with her other hand and realized she was holding a piece of paper. She pulled out her flashlight and shone it on the scrap. Written in the same printing as the note that had directed her to the stable were the words "Does this answer your questions? Get off the ranch or you'll wake up dead."

Nancy stuffed the note into her jeans pocket and staggered to her feet. For a few moments she leaned against the wall, fighting nausea. When she felt better, she walked unsteadily toward the doorway, her flashlight in her hand.

Outside, she heard something near the corner of the stable, and she swung her light in that direction. A figure was just hurrying around the corner of the stable—a furtive, stooped figure in a shapeless jacket that she thought she recognized. It looked very much like Joe Bob! Nancy started to go after him, but her head was swimming and she had to grab the building for support while she heard the footsteps fading into the distance. It took all her strength to make it back to her room.

The next morning Nancy's head still throbbed, but she tried to hide the fact that she was in pain. She wore a cheerful yellow cowboy shirt and a bright yellow ribbon tied around her ponytail. She decided there was no point in calling attention to the fact that she'd been fooling around in the stables after dark—or that she'd been careless enough to get herself conked on the head.

Anyway, Nancy thought wryly, as she put on her makeup with extra care, at least now she had some more clues: a handwritten note and a bump on the side of her head, apparently administered by Joe Bob. But neither clue took her a single step closer to finding Catarina.

Nor was there any clue in the faces of the people gathered around the breakfast table: Mr. Reigert was still pale and weak after his illness; Mrs. Reigert glanced nervously at Nancy as she sat down; Mark was curt and uncommunicative; and Gene, who came late and left early, muttered about a problem with a fence. Although Joe Bob had eaten with them the morning before, that day he was nowhere to be seen.

After breakfast Nancy went to the stables to search the spot where she'd been hit. Discovering nothing, she headed for the kitchen, notebook in hand, to talk to Mrs. Arguello. She found her chopping up vegetables for a luncheon soup. Angela was there, too, wearing a colorful red cotton dress with Mexican embroidery on the bodice. At a sharp glance from Mrs. Arguello, however, she dashed out of the kitchen, scarcely speaking to Nancy.

"I'd like to talk to you for a few minutes, if you don't mind," Nancy said to Mrs. Arguello as she perched on a kitchen stool and opened her notebook, scanning the list of questions she had jotted down the night before. "I'd really like to learn more about Mr. Reigert's first family—about Isabel and Catarina. We'll be covering those chapters in the memoirs before long, and I'd like to have the background work done first."

Mrs. Arguello didn't look up. "What is it you wish to know?" she asked warily, her mouth set in a firm, taut line.

"Well, for starters," Nancy asked, "are there

any pictures of Isabel around? In the attic, maybe? In an old photograph album or something?" From a picture of the mother, Nancy might be able to get an idea of what the daughter would look like now—assuming she was still alive.

Mrs. Arguello hesitated, then said briskly, "No. No pictures."

"None at all?" Nancy persisted, disappointed. "That seems a little unusual. Most people keep snapshots of their families." She would ask Mr. Reigert later.

Mrs. Arguello shrugged. She dumped some sliced carrots into a large pot on the stove, but she didn't answer.

"Well, then, what can you tell me about Isabel's family?" Nancy asked, pursuing another line. "Did they visit here often?"

Mrs. Arguello rolled her eyes. "Visit? Why should they visit here, when they had a beautiful *palacio* in Mexico?"

"A *palacio*?" Nancy looked around at the spacious kitchen, double doors opening onto a small, well-tended herb garden. "But this house is pretty palatial itself."

"Maybe now, but not then. When I first came here with Isabel, when she was just married, Senor Reigert had only a poor house with a few rooms. He was rich in land, but his house was not a place for grand visitors."

"Oh! So Mr. Reigert was poor in those days! He

married the daughter of an aristocratic Mexican family, but he didn't have anything to offer her except his land, and the family disapproved. Is that right?"

Mrs. Arguello nodded, the ghost of a smile on her lips. "Isabel, she was a beautiful young girl," the old woman said. Her voice softened and she stared into space as if she were seeing the pages of some forgotten book. "And Senor Reigert was already as old as her father, although he was still very handsome."

"I don't suppose Isabel's parents could have been very happy about the difference in their ages," Nancy said thoughtfully. At last they seemed to be getting somewhere, if only she could keep Mrs. Arguello talking.

"Sí," Mrs. Arguello replied. She spoke almost in a whisper, as if she had forgotten about Nancy and was talking to herself. "Isabel's father, he was not pleased with the marriage his daughter had made. He said she was loco, crazy. But Isabel was not the one to listen to her father. Very willful, she was, and headstrong."

"Like a wild horse," Nancy said, repeating what Mr. Reigert had said earlier. "Couldn't be saddle broken, by love or by will."

Mrs. Arguello nodded and began to chop a stalk of celery. "You are right," she said. "Not by love or by will."

"But why did Isabel go back to Mexico?" Nancy

asked. "Was she taking her daughter to visit her grandparents?"

Mrs. Arguello's mouth tightened. "No. Not for a visit."

"You mean, she was leaving her husband? She was going back to her parents and taking the little girl with her?"

"*Sí.*" The knife flashed. "Isabel loved her little daughter, and she wanted her to be raised as *she* was, as the daughter of an aristocratic family. There was a quarrel—a bad quarrel—and she left. Senor Reigert, his heart nearly broke. But what could he do? When Isabel made up her mind, no one could stop her—not even Senor Reigert."

"And then the plane crashed," Nancy said quietly, touched by the tragedy of the story that was emerging from Mrs. Arguello's memory. "And Isabel was killed." She hesitated, watching Mrs. Arguello closely. "And the little girl? Do you think she died in the crash? Or did something else happen to her?"

Mrs. Arguello looked up. For a moment she hesitated as if she wanted to say something. Then she bent her head again, her black eyes intent on her work.

Nancy waited. But Mrs. Arguello's mouth had resumed its thin, taut line, and it was clear that she was done talking—for the time being. Nancy left the kitchen and walked down the hall toward Mr. Reigert's room, glancing at her watch. It was nearly eleven o'clock and she'd told Mr. Reigert that she would talk with him at ten-thirty that morning.

Nancy reviewed what she had learned so far. After her conversation with Mrs. Arguello, she suspected that the old woman knew something about Catarina—but what? Of all the people on the ranch, Nancy had to admit, Mrs. Arguello seemed the most likely to have information. And Mr. Reigert had said that he'd caught Mrs. Arguello snooping. Was she involved with the kidnappers?

But if Mrs. Arguello *was* involved with the kidnapping, how did Joe Bob fit in? And Mark and Mrs. Reigert both seemed to be hiding something. Nancy had found a tangle of unresolved connections, a tangle that revealed no pattern at all.

The door to Mr. Reigert's office was open a crack and Nancy could hear voices inside. She knocked tentatively, but nobody acknowledged her. She knocked again and the door swung open by itself. Nancy stepped inside.

Mrs. Reigert was standing looking out the window. That day she was wearing a blue-flowered shirt, with a blue bandanna tied around her throat, and a layered denim skirt with a ruffled petticoat. She looked as if she were on her way to a square dance. But even from the back, she didn't look as if she were in the mood for a dance. Her spine was ramrod straight, and her hands were clenched into fists at her sides.

"Absolutely no regard for my feelings," she was saying in an icy voice. "I sent out the invitations for this Thursday's party weeks ago. How was I to know that you were going to get sick again? I simply will not cancel the party. And that's all there is to it."

Nancy glanced at Mr. Reigert, sitting stiffly at his desk. Listening to Mrs. Reigert, Nancy could understand why her husband thought their marriage had been a mistake.

"I wasn't suggesting that you cancel the party," Mr. Reigert said indignantly. "And I'm not sick— I've got an upset stomach, that's all. I just suggested that you think about a menu that might agree with me a little better than spicy Mexican food—"

"That's the trouble around here," Mrs. Reigert interrupted, stamping her foot. "Everybody wants special treatment. I've planned this party around a Mexican theme. There's even going to be a maria-chi band. And now you—"

"Oh, go ahead with your plans," Mr. Reigert said resignedly. "I don't care what you do. I'll talk to Mrs. Arguello about making something different for me, so I don't have to eat that spicy stuff you're serving."

Mrs. Reigert suddenly softened. "That's a

sweet old dear," she cooed, her voice dripping honey. "I knew you'd think of something. And you'll have a wonderful time, just wait and—" She looked up and saw Nancy.

"Oh, hello, Nancy," she said brightly. "I didn't hear you come in."

"Mr. Reigert asked me to see him at ten-thirty," Nancy explained. "I was already late, and the door pushed open, so I thought I should—"

"Would you mind letting us finish?" Mrs. Reigert asked. "We just have a few more details to firm up about a *fabulous* party we're planning. It's just two days away." She smiled, patting her husband's shoulder. "And, of course, we want *you* to come, too, don't we, dear?" She threw Nancy a sideways glance. "That is, if you're still here."

Mr. Reigert nodded. "Yes," he said, "by all means. Come to the party." He looked at his watch and then turned to Nancy. "I know we agreed to work this morning, but I think we should postpone it until later this afternoon. I have some business to take care of when Mrs. Reigert and I are through talking, and it's going to take awhile." He shot her a meaningful look. "I know you have plenty to do on your own— background research and so forth. I'm sure you're collecting all sorts of useful information."

"Of course," Nancy said, turning to leave the room. Disappointed, she went into the hallway

41

where she caught a flash of red skirt disappearing around the corner. Nancy knew immediately who it was. Had Angela just been passing by, or had she been spying? Nancy had to find out.

"Angela!" she called, rushing after her. She rounded the corner—and found the hallway empty.

Chapter
Five

NANCY WASN'T EVEN sure the fleeing figure had been Angela, but she decided to confront her anyway. If the housemaid was spying on the Reigerts, Nancy needed to know why.

Nancy found Angela in the dining room, calmly setting the table. Had she been there all along or had she raced into the room just ahead of Nancy? She did seem to be breathing rather fast.

Nancy decided that the best way to find out was to be direct about it. "I want to talk to you, Angela," she said. "I want to know if you were listening outside Mr. Reigert's door."

"No comprendo," the girl said. Then she rattled

off something incomprehensible in rapid Spanish. Her dark eyes flashed and her shoulders were straight and proud.

Nancy grabbed her arm. "Wait a minute," she said. "I thought you spoke English. You spoke to me the day I arrived."

"No comprendo," Angela repeated stubbornly. She tried to pull her arm free from Nancy's firm grasp.

Nancy tightened her grip. "I am not going to hurt you, Angela," she said in a reasonable tone, trying to ease the girl's obvious apprehension. "I only want to know if you were listening outside Mr. Reigert's office. Tell me."

The girl stood up straighter and looked at Nancy almost arrogantly. "I do not wish to tell you anything," she said in perfect English. "What I do is none of your affair." She looked haughtily at Nancy's hand on her arm. "Please take your hand off me," she commanded.

Shocked, Nancy let go. The voice she was hearing certainly didn't sound like the voice of a housemaid.

"What's going on here?" Gene asked, coming into the room. He glanced at Angela, and Nancy saw something like a spark of electricity pass between them. "What's the matter?"

Nancy whirled around. "Oh—nothing," she said, deciding that it would be better not to mention her confrontation with Angela. If her instincts were right, something was going on between Gene and Angela. When Nancy turned back to Angela, the girl had slipped out of the room.

It was early afternoon, and Nancy was on her way to the corral, equipped with binoculars and a camera with a telephoto lens. At lunch she had asked Joe Bob to saddle a horse for her.

"Where are you off to this afternoon?" Mark had asked with a sharp look, overhearing her request from across the table.

"I've decided to get to the bottom of this mystery-animal business," Nancy said lightly. She couldn't imagine that the animal had anything to do with the missing heiress, but her natural curiosity was prompting her to find out what was going on. Anyway, at that point, one lead seemed as promising as another, since nothing about the case made much sense.

She glanced at Gene and Mark, measuring their response. "You two seemed to think I'd lost my mind when I told you that I'd seen a spotted deer with antlers."

"It's not your mind you're losing," Gene said emphatically, biting into a taco. "Just your eyesight."

"Personally, I do happen to think you're crazy," Mark growled at Nancy. "Nobody ever saw any spotted deer around here."

Nancy smiled. Mark's charm was beginning to fray a little around the edges. "That's why I'm eager to shoot it," she said. "With my camera, of course. I've never had much to do with guns."

"I hope you're not planning to go riding alone, my dear," Mrs. Reigert told Nancy. "If Mr. Reigert were here, he would tell you the same thing. This is wild country." She shivered delicately. "There are rattlesnakes everywhere, and wild boar. Anything can happen out there, especially when you're unprepared."

Nancy looked around the table. "I'd be glad for company," she offered. But it seemed that everybody was busy for the afternoon. Mrs. Reigert was working on the party, Mark had to make a trip into Rio Hondo, and Gene had work to do.

Joe Bob had simply shaken his head. Nancy was just as glad. After what had happened in the stables the night before, she didn't relish the idea of an afternoon in the wilds of Texas with Joe Bob. And, anyway, she wanted to be alone to think.

When she reached the corral, she found a horse saddled and waiting for her, its reins looped around a fence post. It wasn't the same mild-mannered palomino she had ridden the day before, but a tall, husky gray with a mottled face. When she climbed into the saddle, the horse reared and gave a bad-tempered whinny, as if to declare that he was the boss.

Nancy clung to the saddle with her knees and finally managed to quiet the horse enough to walk him out of the gate. Obviously, that day's ride was going to be more challenging than that of the day before, she thought as the horse galloped away from the ranch house, intent on setting his own fast pace.

The afternoon was hot, and before long Nancy found herself freely perspiring. Dozens of little gnats buzzed around her, and every so often the gray would toss his head angrily, shaking off the horseflies that landed on his flanks. As Nancy was riding through a dense stand of sage and young mesquite, she realized that cowboys wore chaps for a good reason—to protect their legs from thorns and brambles.

The small canyon where she had glimpsed the spotted buck was cut steeply back into the limestone bluff, Nancy realized when she saw it again. It must be what was referred to as a box canyon, a good place to hide any activity from the curious eyes of others.

The little canyon wasn't very wide, and the opening was screened with a thicket of willows so dense that Nancy couldn't see through them. In fact, she couldn't see much at all from the entrance to the canyon. But what if she rode up on the bluff and looked down *into* the canyon? Maybe then she could see whether or not anything was going on.

Nancy reined her horse in and took her binoculars out of her saddlebag. After looping the reins around the saddle horn, she put the strap around her neck and held the binoculars to her eyes, searching for a trail up the side of the bluff. Impatient, the gray pawed the ground and flicked his tail at the flies.

Crack! Startled, Nancy dropped the binoculars. What she had heard sounded exactly like a high-powered rifle! Its sound echoed through the canyon, and the gray danced nervously to the side.

Bam! That time there was no mistaking it. The bullet thudded into a tree only a few feet from Nancy. Somebody was shooting at her!

Chapter

Six

Nancy didn't have time to worry about the rifle shot, or even to wonder who was shooting at her. She was too busy trying to control her horse. He had decided that it was time to put himself out of harm's way—a *long way* out of harm's way. Eyes rolling in fright, he reared up on his hind legs, nearly throwing Nancy, then took off back across the sagebrush at his fastest gallop, ears back, tail streaming.

Nancy grabbed for the reins, but they were flying loose. The only thing she could do was grip the saddle with her knees, clutch the saddle horn with her hands, and pray that the horse wouldn't step into a prairie dog hole.

Suddenly Nancy heard hoofbeats pounding hard on the rocky ground behind her.

"Hang on, Nancy!" somebody shouted. "I'm coming!" A few seconds later Gene was riding beside her, leaning off his horse to reach for Nancy's loose reins. It was like a stunt in a cowboy movie.

But, while the runaway scene of most westerns ended with the hero clasping the heroine in his arms and reassuring her that everything was all right, this one ended with Gene's demanding, "Just who put you up on Bad Guy? And who was doing all the shooting? Is somebody trying to kill you?"

"What?" Nancy asked, breathing hard. Her binoculars were still dangling from their strap, and she took them off and stuffed them into her saddlebag. She wiped the sweat off her forehead with the back of her hand. "Bad Guy? Who's Bad Guy?"

"This crazy horse," Gene said disgustedly. "That's who." He looped the reins over the gray's neck and Nancy took them up again. "He's the meanest-tempered horse on the ranch. Last year he bucked Mark off and stomped him pretty badly. Who told you to take him? Or did you saddle him up yourself?"

Nancy shook her head. She had the growing suspicion that that day's ride had been sabotaged even before she started out. "At lunch I asked Joe Bob to saddle a horse for me," she told Gene.

"And then I found this one in the corral, already saddled."

"Joe Bob must be getting weak in the head." Gene scowled. "He knows better than to put a newcomer on Bad Guy. I'll have a talk with him." The two of them reined around and began to ride back toward the ranch.

"Was it the gunshot that started him off?" Gene asked. "Did you get a look at whoever was doing the shooting?"

Nancy glanced at Gene's profile, a thought suddenly occurring to her. Maybe *he* had fired the rifle! Maybe he was hiding something in the canyon and wanted to keep her away, or else maybe he wanted her out of the way entirely. She shivered. It would be just as well not to let him know that *she* knew the shots had been fired at her.

"I guess it was the noise that set him off," she said slowly, playing dumb. "Anyway, he just started to run. And, no, I didn't see who was firing the rifle. Whoever it was, he—or she—was too far away."

"Well," said Gene, giving her an approving glance, "you did a mighty good job of hanging on. I was checking fence down in the draw and caught a glimpse of you flying by. When I realized you were on Bad Guy, I figured it was all over. I would've laid odds that we'd be prying you out of a big prickly pear or scraping you off a rock by now." He chuckled. "Not everyone can manage a big horse like this."

Nancy didn't respond to Gene's admiration. She was deep in thought, trying to sort through the things that had happened. Somebody had hit her on the head the night before, and immediately afterward, she thought she had seen Joe Bob ducking around the corner. That afternoon Joe Bob had given her a horse that had a reputation for being impossible to handle. And then somebody had shot at her—with the intention of either scaring her away from the canyon or doing away with her for good.

Was it just luck that Gene had been close by, close enough to stop her runaway horse? It was tempting to speculate that Joe Bob and Gene were working together, Nancy thought. But she hadn't found anything to connect the two of them to the ransom notes or to Catarina herself. And Mr. Reigert had insisted that Gene was the only one on the ranch who could be trusted. Was he wrong?

When they got back to the ranch, just before four o'clock, Gene went to the stables to find Joe Bob, and Nancy went to Mr. Reigert's office to question him about Gene's background.

"Gene Newsom's worked for me for the last four years," Mr. Reigert said firmly in answer to Nancy's first question. "I knew his daddy for forty years, and I've known Gene ever since he was a kid in diapers. If you think he's got anything to do with this ransom business, you're dropping your loop on the wrong calf. Gene doesn't have it in him to think a dishonest thought."

Nancy scrutinized Mr. Reigert's stern face. He certainly believed what he was saying, and there wasn't anything concrete to connect Gene with the gunshot—except for the fact that he'd been in the immediate vicinity. The night before, however, she had *seen* the back of Joe Bob's shapeless old coat disappearing around the corner.

"Well, then, what about Joe Bob?" she asked. "Do you trust him?"

Mr. Reigert laughed. "Joe Bob? He's Gene's man. He'd never do anything that Gene didn't approve of."

Nancy frowned. That meant that if Joe Bob had hit her on the head or intended her to ride Bad Guy, he'd done it with Gene's approval. Hearing a knock at the door, she turned to see Gene walking into the room.

"There you are," he said to Nancy with a grin. "I thought I'd find you here."

"Nancy was just asking about—" Mr. Reigert began.

"About the different people who work at the ranch," Nancy interrupted with a warning glance at Mr. Reigert. "I thought it might be helpful for my work if I knew a little bit about their backgrounds."

"Well, if it's Joe Bob you're asking about, I'm the one who can tell you," Gene said gruffly, pulling up a chair and straddling it. "He showed up here a couple of years ago, broke and out of work. I don't know where he came from, but I do know one thing—he's the best horse man in these parts. He really knows his animals." Gene shook his head.

"And, by the way, he says he *didn't* saddle Bad Guy for you, Nancy. He says he saddled up the palomino mare. He did it right after lunch and left her in the corral." Gene frowned. "Looks like we've got a mystery on our hands. Who switched those horses?"

"What's this about Bad Guy?" Mr. Reigert asked sharply. "Somebody been fooling with that horse again? I thought I left orders—"

"It's all right, Mr. Reigert," Gene said. "Nancy rode him out today and he ran away with her. But it turned out okay in the end. Nancy managed to stay on board while I caught up with her." He grinned. "Bad Guy must be slowing down a little in his old age. When he dumped Mark, he wouldn't let *anybody* catch him."

Nancy stared at Gene. If Joe Bob hadn't saddled up Bad Guy, who had? Of course, it was possible that Joe Bob was lying, or that Gene was lying—or both. As a matter of fact, she added to herself, *anything* was possible.

In terms of the case, Nancy had five suspects— six, if she counted Angela—and nothing to indicate how *any* of them were connected to the kidnapping. *If* there was a kidnapping, she reminded herself. Maybe the ransom notes were hoaxes.

Gene turned back to Mr. Reigert. "Actually, I stopped in to ask whether you're going to be needing Nancy tomorrow night. The rodeo starts in Rio Hondo, and it occurred to me that she might enjoy it."

"By all means," Mr. Reigert said. "You two go and have yourselves a fine time."

"But—" Nancy started to protest. She wasn't sure it was a good idea for her to go out alone with Gene, at least until she had a clearer idea about what had happened that day. Anyway, she had plenty of detective work to do at the ranch—and a trip to the rodeo surely wasn't going to help her search for clues. However, Mr. Reigert didn't give her a chance to say no.

"No buts," Mr. Reigert said stubbornly. "You do what Gene says."

"Thanks," Gene replied, getting to his feet. "Be ready about six," he told Nancy. "It's a forty-minute drive to Rio Hondo." He grinned engagingly. "And wear your jeans and boots," he added. "After all, it's a rodeo."

Mr. Reigert glanced at the clock. It was nearly four-thirty. "Gene, speaking of Rio Hondo, I want you to drive to town with me this evening. Al Patterson's agreed to talk about selling me that new Brahma bull of his."

Gene brightened. "Sure thing," he said. "That's good news." He turned to Nancy. "You want to ride to Rio Hondo and watch a couple of old cowmen haggle over a bull?" he asked.

Nancy couldn't help smiling. "I think I'll pass on that one," she said. "I've had enough excitement for one day."

By the time Nancy climbed out of a hot bath and into her velvety pink nightgown that night, the day's events were beginning to take their toll—especially the jolting ride on Bad Guy. Every joint was stiff and her muscles were complaining bitterly.

But she couldn't go to sleep just yet. She needed to talk to Ned. She needed to hear his voice and know that he was thinking about her. And she needed his ideas. Working alone—especially in a situation where there didn't seem to be many leads—was terribly frustrating.

Ned listened while Nancy told him what had happened since she had talked to him the night before: the crack on the head, the gunshot and the ride at breakneck speed on Bad Guy, and the encounter with Angela.

After a minute he said, "I don't like the sound of things down there, Nancy." There was a note of real worry in his voice. "You could be in serious danger. You don't even know who to trust."

"Oh, I don't think there's much danger," she said as lightly as she could. "The real problem is not being able to put any of this stuff together. There are the ransom notes, and the notes I received last night, which are in an entirely different print. Now there's a horse that nobody saddled and a gunshot that might or might not have been accidental.

"Something else puzzles me, too, and that's the way Angela behaved this morning. I have the feeling that she's a rather unusual housemaid. But none of this points to the whereabouts of Catarina —that is, *if* the girl's still alive."

"You think the kidnapping might be a hoax, designed to trick Mr. Reigert out of the ransom money?"

"It's entirely possible," Nancy said. "Anyway, there hasn't been any evidence yet that would indicate that Catarina is alive. All we have is an old scrap of cloth and a baby shoe."

"Listen, Nancy," Ned said, "I don't have any classes for the next few days. How about if I fly down and give you a hand?"

Nancy sighed and closed her eyes, thinking how wonderful it would be to have Ned with her. It would be too difficult to explain his presence on the ranch, but maybe he *could* help her in a different way—if he was willing, of course.

"If you want to help," she said, "maybe you could go to Dallas and see what you can learn about Jonelle and Mark Blake." Quickly she filled him in on everything she already knew about the pair. "It seems like a long shot," she admitted. "And I'm not sure it's worth making a trip to Dallas just to—"

"I'll be on my way first thing in the morning," Ned said eagerly. "I'm sure I can stay with my uncle. In fact, he'll probably be eager to help out. Maybe he can lend me a hand with the investigating." He gave her his uncle's phone number. "Better give me a little time to see what I can dig up before you call me."

"Wonderful," Nancy said enthusiastically. Dallas wasn't very close, but it was a lot closer than Emerson College, and she felt better just knowing that Ned wanted to help. Their relationship had been uncertain for a long time, and his concern meant a lot to her.

Suddenly an enormous yawn overtook her. "I'm really tired, Ned, and I ache all over. I'd better call it a night."

"Take care of yourself, Drew," Ned said tenderly. "Stay away from wild horses and dark stables. And hang in there."

"Thanks, Nickerson," Nancy said, smiling a little. "I'll try."

When she had hung up the phone, Nancy went back to her notebook to review the situation once more. But even though the questions posed by the case were intriguing, she couldn't keep her eyes open. Drowsily, she got up to check the door and make sure that it was locked, then she turned off the light and instantly fell asleep.

But she didn't stay asleep for long. The lighted face of the clock beside her bed read eleven when she heard a hand fumbling at her locked door. She was wide awake immediately.

The full moon shining through the window gave just enough light for her to see that the door handle was turning, and she could hear the metallic clink of a key in the lock. Somebody had just unlocked the door of her room!

Chapter

Seven

THE DOOR SWUNG open slowly, creaking ominously, as Nancy sat up in bed, her heart pounding. In the moonlight that streamed through the window, she saw the shadowy bulk of a man.

"Nancy Drew!" a voice spoke from the doorway. "Are you awake?"

"I am now," Nancy said, getting up and pulling on her pink robe. Mr. Reigert stepped into the room. "What's happened?" she asked.

"This," Mr. Reigert grunted, thrusting something at Nancy.

"What is it?" Nancy asked. She went to the window and pulled the curtains tight before she

60

turned on the bedside light. Mr. Reigert had handed her the plastic case of a videocassette!

"Come to my bedroom and I'll show you what's on that tape," he said, sounding tense.

Nancy followed Mr. Reigert down the dark hall, clutching the cassette in her hands. When they reached his room, he closed and locked the door.

"Sit down," he commanded. He went to the VCR and inserted the tape. "I found this in my office," he said, "after I got back from Rio Hondo. It was wrapped in that." He gestured toward some brown paper crumpled up on the floor.

Nancy examined the wrapping paper. Mr. Reigert's name was printed on it in large block letters, with what looked like a crayon. But other than that, there was nothing.

Nancy looked up as the screen showed the full-color image of a young woman seated in a chair, her hands tied behind her back and her ankles lashed together. Her straight dark hair hung down over her shoulders and her thickly lashed brown eyes were wide with fear. She was wearing a full blue cotton skirt and a ruffled peasant blouse. She seemed to be struggling against the ropes, trying to get free.

"Now do you believe that we have your daughter?" a deep male voice asked through the VCR. "And just in case you're not sure that this is your daughter, look at this." The image of the girl vanished and another appeared in its place—a photograph of a beautiful young woman, dark haired and dark eyed, wearing a lacy white dress. Beside her, one arm wrapped protectively around her shoulders, stood Mr. Reigert.

"That's Isabel," Mr. Reigert said in a strangled voice, staring at the screen. The woman in the photograph and the bound girl on the tape looked quite similar. "It's the only picture I kept."

"But Mrs. Arguello said that there weren't any pictures," Nancy said, surprised.

"I destroyed all the others. But this photograph was taken on our wedding day." He nodded toward the dresser. "I kept it hidden in the bottom drawer of that chest."

"It's gone?"

"Yes." The answer was an anguished whisper. Mr. Reigert kept his eyes on the screen.

"Who do you think—?"

"Maybe Mrs. Arguello," Mr. Reigert said. "Or maybe my wife." His voice was bitter. "She's always poking around in here."

Nancy looked back at the screen. The wedding picture had been replaced by another, this one a snapshot of Isabel holding a small child, both waving at the camera.

"And this picture?" Nancy asked.

"It appeared in the local paper two days after I got word of the crash," Mr. Reigert said dully. "It had been taken a few weeks before Isabel left. That's the same dress Catarina was wearing on the day she left with her mother, and those are the shoes with the bells on the laces. That outfit was her favorite."

Mr. Reigert's eyes were glued to the screen, where the image of the girl appeared once again. This time her struggles were more violent. On the floor in front of her lay a gun.

"Now you know we mean business," the man said menacingly. "We'll kill your daughter if you don't pay up. Get the money from the bank—half a million in unmarked bills. Then we'll tell you how to hand it over. When we have the money, you get the girl."

The camera zoomed in on the girl's terrified face, and she began to speak.

"Please, Father!" she pleaded. "If you don't pay, they're going to kill me! Do as they say—I beg you! Pay them the money!" The screen went black.

For a long time Mr. Reigert sat in silence. "Tomorrow I'm going into town to get the money," he said finally. "I'll see Sam Lawson, president of the bank."

"So you're convinced that that girl is your daughter?" Nancy asked.

"I *know* she is," Mr. Reigert replied. He rubbed his forehead. "Can't you see the resemblance?"

"Yes, they do look alike. But makeup can do wonders," Nancy pointed out. "For all we know, the whole thing could be a hoax." She thought for a minute. "Does Catarina have any distinguishing characteristics? Any birthmarks?"

"As a matter of fact," Mr. Reigert said reflectively, "she does. A small strawberry-shaped mark on the inside of her right ankle."

"That's it!" Nancy exclaimed excitedly. "That'll be our test! Now, if we can get in contact with the people who claim to be the kidnappers, we can refuse to pay up unless they show us her birthmark. If they can't, or if they show us one that's *wrong,* we'll refuse to pay."

Mr. Reigert stared at Nancy. "Yes, that's exactly what we'll do. They're bound to contact us to give us instructions about how to pay the money. Instead of giving the money to them, we can demand that they show us Catarina's birthmark."

Nancy gave a frustrated sigh. "Yes, but that's only the first step," she said. "If they prove that the girl *is* your daughter, we still won't have any way of knowing where she's being held. We have no way of finding her—unless we pay the ransom."

"I won't take chances with her life," Mr. Reigert said. "If the birthmark proves that the girl on the tape is Catarina, I'm going to hand over the money." He shook his head. "But it's going to take every penny I have."

"Every penny?" Nancy asked in surprise. "But I thought—"

"You thought that I was a wealthy man? Have

you looked at oil prices lately, Nancy? Or the price of beef? This ransom is going to undo me. There won't be a nickel left. *That* ought to surprise my wife and her good-for-nothing son!"

Nancy stood up. "Mr. Reigert," she said firmly, "if we discover that the girl *is* your daughter, we'll know that we're dealing with real kidnappers. It will be time to call in the police."

Mr. Reigert looked up, his eyes flashing. "Over my dead body!" he said. "Billy McPhee is the sheriff of this county. How he got to be sheriff is anybody's guess—probably bought the job at the county courthouse. I grew up with that snaggle-toothed old coot and I don't trust him. That's why I brought *you* into the case! Billy couldn't deduce his way out of a paper bag!"

He glared at her. "And if you don't think you can handle it, Nancy Drew, pack up and get off my ranch! Right now!"

Nancy was sorely tempted to do exactly what Mr. Reigert suggested—pack her bags and leave. But she'd never been one to run from a challenge, no matter how frustrating, and she'd certainly never left a client high and dry in the middle of an extortion attempt. She shook her head. "I'm here and I'm staying," she said. "I want to find Catarina."

Mr. Reigert nodded. "Good. But you've got your work cut out for you. Looks like things are coming to a head pretty quick."

* * *

All the next day Nancy tried to dig deeper into the mystery. She studied the tape again, paying careful attention to the picture of Isabel. Something about it seemed vaguely familiar, but she couldn't put her finger on it, no matter how long she stared at it.

She had another unsatisfactory conversation with Mrs. Reigert and a frustrating half hour with Mark, who just kept grunting noncommittally in answer to her more and more pointed questions about his earlier life.

She talked with Mrs. Arguello again, trying to discover if she had taken the picture from Mr. Reigert's drawer. But she got nowhere. Mrs. Arguello was obviously not going to talk.

Gene was out somewhere on ranch business and he'd taken Joe Bob with him. That left only the other ranch hands, who never came into the house, and Angela, whom Nancy couldn't find anywhere. She could only hope that Ned would find out something in Dallas.

Without anything more to do, Nancy saddled up the palomino mare and started off in the direction of the box canyon. In the back of her mind was the idea that something might be going on there. She wasn't sure what, but it was worth a try. If she rode up to the top of the bluff and looked down, she might be able to spot something.

Unfortunately, just as she was getting ready to turn off the main trail to head toward the bluffs, she was hit by a sudden downpour. In Texas, she knew, they called those rainstorms gully-washers or frog-chokers. But even though the names given to them were funny, there was nothing humorous about the danger of flash floods they posed.

Letting the palomino have her head, she galloped back to the ranch, soaked to the skin and terribly frustrated. It had not been a productive afternoon.

However, after she had had a shower, washed her hair, and put on a fresh pair of jeans and a shirt, Nancy felt better. She decided to call Ned. It was almost four and still raining hard. She wasn't sure that Gene would want to drive to the rodeo that evening, but in case he did, Nancy wanted to talk to Ned first. She dialed Ned's uncle, hearing the crackle of static on the line from the electrical storm outside.

"It's great to know that you're only a few hundred miles away," Ned said when he answered the phone. "This separation stuff is for the birds, Nan."

Nancy smiled softly. "I know," she said. "I hope your day has been more productive than mine."

Ned paused. "I haven't found out much," he admitted. "Jonelle went to work at the Plaza Balcones Club on June tenth last year. She gave her name as Jonelle Blake. But since she only worked for six weeks or so—she quit at the end of July to marry Mr. Reigert—the club didn't keep her application on file. No one there remembers her. And I haven't been able to find any trace of a woman using the name Jonelle Blake."

Nancy sighed. "I'm not surprised," she said. "Maybe we're barking up the wrong tree."

"I don't think so," Ned replied. "My uncle Al says he remembers something about a woman named Jonelle—it's not exactly a common name. We're going to do some more digging." His voice deepened. "Any more problems out there?"

"Not really," Nancy said. She brought Ned up to date on the events since their last conversation. "Frankly," she added, "I'm getting a little concerned about the progress of this case. I'm afraid—"

Suddenly there was a brilliant flash of lightning outside Nancy's window, followed immediately by an enormous clap of thunder and a splintering crash. Nancy gave an involuntary shriek as the light on her bedside table suddenly went dark. Then she laughed shakily.

"Sorry, Ned," she said. "It was just a bolt of lightning . . . Ned? Ned?"

But there wasn't any use in trying to talk to Ned. The phone was dead. The lightning had apparently knocked out the telephone lines.

"What? Miss the rodeo?" Gene had said when Nancy asked if they were going to drive through the rain to Rio Hondo. "No way." They asked Mark if he wanted to go with them, but he mumbled something about an errand in town and climbed into his Cadillac and drove off alone.

The Rio Hondo rodeo was held in a huge barnlike arena cooled by big overhead fans. The dirt floor was surrounded by wooden bleachers behind a high metal fence. At one end an announcer's stand was draped in colorful bunting. The first event of the evening was the bucking bronco ride, and Nancy and Gene watched it while eating hot dogs lathered with mustard and catsup.

"Watch closely," Gene said, pointing toward a wooden chute. "They've put Mike Malory up on Old Blue. That pair is the best in the business."

Nancy held her breath as one of the gates opened and a milky blue horse exploded into the arena. The blue-shirted cowboy was gripping the saddle horn with one hand, the other arm flung high, spurred heels lifted against the horse's muscular shoulders. The horse bucked viciously.

"Wow," Gene said admiringly. "Looks like Blue is giving Mike some ride. You see, in this event, it's sort of a partnership between horse and rider. All the cowboys draw for their horses before the event. Everybody hopes to get a tough horse because a tougher horse gets you higher points. You're scored on the way you time your spurring action with the bucking pattern of the horse."

In less than ten seconds the ride was all over. The pickup man rode alongside the bucking horse, and Mike Malory swung easily off Old Blue and onto the other horse. A clown in a ragged red shirt and bulky overalls danced out into the arena and waved his arms at the loose bronco, herding him expertly through an open gate.

Gene touched Nancy's arm. "See that clown?" he asked. "That's Joe Bob. When the rodeo's in town, he can't stay away. He's got to come do his clown act. And there's none better. He can handle a wild bull or a mad stallion like they were toys."

Nancy stared. The clown in the ring moved around the dangerous horse with quickness and grace. She'd never have guessed that he was the slow, stooped Joe Bob.

Gene glanced at her curiously. "How do you like it so far?" he asked.

"Terrific!" Nancy exclaimed. "But what goes on back there?" she asked, pointing to the back of the arena.

Gene stood up. "Let's go see," he suggested. "We've got time before the next event."

Nancy followed Gene around the arena and behind the fence. The area was filled with wooden chutes and fences and crowded with livestock and milling cowboys.

Gene beckoned. "Here's something you ought to see," he said. "Climb up on this fence and take a close look at Tom Boy. Some people say he's the meanest bull in captivity."

With the cowboys milling around her, Nancy climbed to the top of the wooden fence. Tom Boy was a giant red bull with a huge hump on his back and wicked-looking horns. Nancy looked at him apprehensively as he rolled his eyes and tossed his head, pawing the dust with pointed hooves.

Nancy was clinging to the top of the fence, looking over, when she felt a hand on her back. She was about to turn around when the hand pushed, hard, and she found herself falling over the fence into Tom Boy's stall!

Chapter

Eight

Nancy grabbed at the wooden fence as she went over the top, trying to save herself, but it was no use. In the next instant she was flat on her back in the stall, staring up in horror at Tom Boy, who loomed over her like an enormous red mountain. For a split second he stood frozen, as surprised as she was. Then he lowered his horns with a rumbling bawl and began to charge.

Nancy managed to scramble to her feet, but the huge bull caught her leather belt with one sharp horn and lifted her up, flinging her against the side of the stall and knocking the breath out of her. Nancy fell back to the dirt in a heap, gasping for air, while Tom Boy, bellowing, backed up for another try.

Suddenly there was a hubbub of frantic activity in the pen. A cowboy opened a metal gate that led into another stall and two others dropped loops of rope over Tom Boy's head and began to yank him toward the gate. A fourth jumped over the fence and tossed Nancy over his shoulder as if she were a sack of flour. The next thing she knew, she was safely on the ground outside the stall, and Gene was kneeling beside her, white faced and shaken.

"Are you okay?" he asked, helping her sit up.

Nancy nodded, rubbing her shoulder where Tom Boy had slammed her against the fence. There was a rip in her shirt and the skin was beginning to bleed. "Just a little banged up, that's all."

She looked around. The cowboy who had pulled her out of the stall had disappeared before she could thank him. She glanced at Gene. He acted as if he was worried about her—but why hadn't he jumped into the stall to help her, as the others had?

She remembered the hand on her back. Somebody had pushed her into Tom Boy's pen! Gene? Had he *intended* that she be attacked by the bull?

"What happened?" Gene asked, bending over to examine the bloody scrape on her shoulder. "How did you fall?"

"I didn't fall," Nancy replied curtly, wincing as his fingers touched raw skin. "I was pushed."

"Pushed!" Gene's mouth fell open and he sat back on his heels, staring at her. If he was faking surprise, Nancy thought, he was doing a pretty good job of it.

After a moment he shook his head. "I don't believe that anyone would deliberately push you," he said flatly, his eyes never leaving her face. "Who would do such a crazy thing?"

The cowboy who had opened the gate appeared beside them then, his hands in his pockets. "She was pushed, all right," he told Gene. "I saw the whole thing. It was one of the rodeo clowns, but I'll be blessed if I know which one. They all look alike with that clown makeup on."

Gene looked up. "How'd it happen?" he asked.

The cowboy shrugged. "You'd turned around to talk to somebody else, and he just stepped up behind her and gave her a good shove. The next thing I knew, she was lying on the ground in Tom Boy's stall." He shook his head wonderingly. "That bull is one mean beast. She's lucky she's not dead."

A rodeo clown! Nancy's mind raced. Joe Bob was a rodeo clown! He had almost certainly tried to put her out of commission earlier. And if Mr. Reigert was right, Joe Bob would only operate on orders from Gene! Had the two of them engineered *this* attempt on her life, expecting to pass it off as an accident?

Gene looked at her with a frown. "I can guess what you're thinking, Nancy," he said, shaking his head as he helped her stand up. "You're dead wrong. Rodeo clown or no rodeo clown, it wasn't Joe Bob who pushed you. I don't know who it was or why he did it, but it wasn't Joe Bob. I'd stake my life on that."

Nancy wanted to believe Gene. But why hadn't he jumped into the pen to help her?

That question was still uppermost in Nancy's thoughts as she and Gene drove silently back to the ranch. Her puzzling was interrupted, however. Gene had some questions for *her*.

"I'm kind of interested in what you do for a living, Nancy," he said casually as they drove along. The rain had stopped, and the clouds had cleared out, leaving a beautifully clear, moonlit night. "What sorts of things have you written? You look kind of young to have had much of a career as a writer."

Nancy shrugged. "Writing's like anything else," she said, trying to evade his question. Did he suspect that she wasn't a writer? "Sometimes you hit it lucky. I guess that's what's happened to me."

"But *what* have you written?" Gene persisted. He turned off the main road, onto the lane that led to Casa del Alamo. The silver moonlight that flooded the open rangeland was so bright that they almost didn't need the headlights. "Do you have any best-sellers?"

"No, no best-sellers," Nancy said, pausing to invent. "Mostly I do—crime reporting, for newspapers. A detective story or two. And of course I do ghostwriting, like the job I'm doing for Mr. Reigert."

"I see." Gene was silent for a moment. "How did you two get connected? I mean, it seems a little unlikely that Mr. Reigert just opened up the telephone book and found you."

Nancy looked at him, convinced that something more than casual curiosity was behind his questions. "Somebody recommended me," she said uncomfortably.

"Oh? Who?"

"Well—it was—" Nancy stammered. Suddenly she was hit by an inspiration. "It was an acquaintance who's a reporter for one of the Dallas newspapers. I guess Mr. Reigert must have met him when he was in Dal—"

"Hey, look!" Gene interrupted her excitedly. The truck lurched to a screeching halt as Gene put on the brakes.

"What?" Nancy cried, looking around.

"Over there!" Gene exclaimed. He pointed toward a shadowy clump of trees, then rubbed his eyes. "I can't believe it! I can't believe what I've just seen."

"What is it?" Nancy demanded. "I don't see anything."

Gene shook his head unbelievingly. "I must be going crazy," he muttered. "Maybe it's the full moon."

"But what did you see?"

Gene rubbed his eyes again. "It was a kangaroo!"

Chapter

Nine

THE NEXT MORNING Nancy watched Joe Bob closely as he ate his breakfast. If he had been the one who pushed her into Tom Boy's stall, his face certainly didn't reveal it. He looked as impassive as ever, his eyes fixed on the rapidly disappearing stack of pancakes on the plate in front of him.

But Gene wasn't at all impassive. He was reporting what he had seen the night before as they drove down the lane in the moonlight.

"Big kangaroo, about waist high," he was telling Mark excitedly. "It was just hopping along." He shook his head. "I know this isn't Australia, but I swear I saw it."

Mark was staring at Gene, and Nancy thought she saw fear in Mark's eyes for a moment. But then it disappeared as quickly, and Mark was his ordinary self.

"You're as crazy as Nancy," he said emphatically, with a glance in her direction. "There may be a kangaroo or two in the zoo in San Antonio, but they certainly don't run around loose in this part of the country." He grinned wickedly. "Are you sure that you and Nancy weren't hitting the firewater last night?"

Gene shook his head and pushed his chair back. "Nope. I don't know what happened to it, but it's out there somewhere, and I intend to find it." He stood up and reached for his hat. "Want to ride out with me this morning, Nancy?"

Nancy shook her head. "No, thanks," she said. "I need to work with Mr. Reigert." In the bright morning light, her questions about Gene's honesty and Joe Bob's complicity had been revived. It was time to tell Mr. Reigert about the attempts on her life and hear his thoughts on the matter.

Mrs. Reigert put down her coffee cup. "I'm afraid there won't be any work this morning, Nancy," she said. "It's his stomach again, poor dear. He couldn't even eat any breakfast." She frowned. "Wouldn't you know it? He *would* have to get sick on the day of the party."

"He's sick?" Nancy asked worriedly, pushing back her plate. "Again?"

Mark looked at her. "Chronic condition. And he's always in a foul mood when he gets sick. You'd best leave him alone."

Nancy stood up. "I think I'll just look in on him," she said. "We have quite a bit of work."

Mr. Reigert was still in bed. His eyes were shut and his cheeks had a greenish tinge that Nancy didn't like at all. She stood beside the bed for a moment, looking down at him.

"How are you feeling?" she asked.

"Awful," Mr. Reigert said without opening his eyes. "And it doesn't get any better when I think about Jonelle. She's sure to say that I'm doing this on purpose, to spoil her party."

"You've got to let us call a doctor," Nancy said.

Mr. Reigert's eyes flew open. "Nonsense," he exclaimed, his voice sounding stronger. "I'm not sick enough to let some beetle-brained doctor go poking at me. And, anyway, what can he tell me? I already know that I've got a stomachache.

"It's funny, I haven't eaten any garlic lately, but I've got this odd taste of garlic in my mouth." He raised himself up on his elbow, picked up the water glass on his bedside table, and took a swallow. "Just can't seem to get rid of it.

"Anyway, Nancy, I've got an errand for you. I don't feel up to going in to Rio Hondo to the bank this morning. You've got to get the money and bring it back here."

Nancy swallowed. "Get the money? Pick up half a million dollars in cash?"

Mr. Reigert eyed her. "Of course. Don't detectives have assignments like this every now and then? Hand me the phone. If they've got the lines fixed, I'll call Sam Lawson, let him know you're coming, and tell him to hand the money over to you today."

The lines were apparently repaired, because Mr. Reigert began to dial the phone. "Go tell that wife of mine that you're running an errand for me in town and you need a car."

"I still wish you'd let me call the doctor," Nancy said.

"No doctor," Mr. Reigert grunted. "Now get out of here and get on with your detective work."

Mrs. Reigert seemed extremely curious when Nancy told her that she had to go to town and needed to borrow a car. After a few minutes of questioning, though, she must have realized that she wasn't going to get any information out of Nancy and she gave up.

Nancy left with the strong feeling that Mrs. Reigert didn't trust her. Just before Nancy left, she saw Mrs. Reigert going into her husband's room with a determined look on her face. If she couldn't get the information out of Nancy, apparently she was going to try to get it out of her husband.

Before she left the house, Nancy called Ned at his uncle's in Dallas, but there wasn't any answer. She hoped Ned was having better luck with his investigations in Dallas than she was having at Casa del Alamo.

Nancy decided that she'd better wear something other than jeans for her visit to the bank. She put on the khaki skirt and blazer she had worn on the plane and added a silky brown print blouse.

At the bank she was ushered into Sam Lawson's office as soon as she gave her name. It was a small-town bank, and Mr. Lawson's office was sparsely furnished, unlike the plush offices of the city banks with which Nancy was familiar.

Like his office, Mr. Lawson was spare and lean. Nancy guessed that he was about the same age as Mr. Reigert. Leaning back in his chair, he stretched out his legs and carefully appraised Nancy over his gold-rimmed glasses. She saw that he was wearing cowboy boots. He didn't look much like her idea of a bank president.

"I want you to drive on back to that ranch, Nancy Driscoll," he commanded brusquely, "and tell Bob Reigert he has to give me more time to get the money together."

Nancy was taken aback. "More time? But why?"

Mr. Lawson frowned. "I don't know where Bob gets the idea that he can just up and pull half a million dollars out of this small bank on half a day's notice. Doesn't he know that we don't keep that much money on hand? The armored car is coming out from San Antonio late this afternoon. I won't have it until after five o'clock."

"I thought that he called you for the money."

"Oh, he called, all right. But he didn't say exactly when he wanted the money. I assumed that he'd want it tomorrow. By the way, what did you say that he wants the money for? And who are you that he'd trust you with that kind of money?"

"I *didn't* say why he wanted it," Nancy answered pointedly. If Mr. Reigert had wanted Sam Lawson to know, he would have told him. "And as for me, I'm a writer. I'm helping him write his memoirs."

Sam Lawson hooted with laughter. "His memoirs? There are going to be some mighty uncomfortable people around these parts, once they hear about this. Bob Reigert knows a lot of dirt about a lot of people—and, unfortunately, all of it's true."

Nancy smiled. "I don't think he intends to tell *those* kinds of stories," she said. She brought Mr. Lawson back to the point of their conversation. "But he really did insist on having the money today, and no later. It can't wait until tomorrow."

Mr. Lawson gave her an irritated look. "I'll have to talk to him myself, of course," he replied testily. "But he'll have it today. In fact, I'll bring it out myself later, since this seems to be so important."

"Oh, I suppose you're coming to Mrs. Reigert's party, then," Nancy said.

"No, I am *not* coming to Mrs. Reigert's party," the president said firmly.

He pulled his feet back and sat up straight in his chair. "There's something about her that I just don't . . . Well, let's just say I invented an excuse not to come to the party."

"Did you know Mrs. Reigert before they were married?" Nancy asked.

"No, and nobody else did either," Mr. Lawson answered. Nancy looked surprised, so Mr. Lawson continued to explain. "I looked into her background out of curiosity. It seems she appeared at that club out of nowhere, just the week before Bob went up for a visit. He always stays there when he goes to Dallas on business."

"Appeared out of nowhere?"

"That's what I said, isn't it? Nobody had ever heard of Jonelle whatever-her-name-was before she got that job. It was like she'd just dropped out of the sky."

He shook his head. "I don't know why, but I don't trust that woman, or that rattlesnake son of hers." He began to rustle some papers. "Now, why don't you get on back to the ranch and tell Bob what I said."

Nancy stood up, disappointed. For a moment she had thought that she might get some real information out of Mr. Lawson. "What time can we expect you tonight?" she asked.

"There'll be too many people around during the

evening, so I'll come out later," Mr. Lawson said. "Around midnight. I'll just have to tell Bob that's the best I can do.

Suddenly something occurred to Nancy. *No one* was to know that Mr. Reigert had taken the money out of the bank. It was too risky. She couldn't let anyone see Mr. Lawson.

"Just to be on the safe side," Nancy said casually, "how about if I ride out to the gate on the main road and meet you with an extra horse. You can ride in with me."

"Ride in?"

"Mr. Reigert wants to keep this a secret. You know how his wife would get if she knew there was half a million dollars lying around. She'd want to spend every penny. So come in by horse. A car's too noisy. You don't want Mrs. Reigert to see you anyway or she'll know you lied about not being able to come to her party," Nancy said with a grin.

Mr. Lawson looked startled. "Oh, that's right," he agreed.

"Good," said Nancy. "I'll be at the gate at midnight with the horses."

The house seemed quiet when Nancy got back from her errand at the bank later that morning. She looked in on Mr. Reigert, to tell him about the meeting with Mr. Lawson, but he was asleep. She went down the hall toward her room, intending to make another call to Ned to learn if there was any information about Mrs. Reigert and her son. As she went past Mrs. Reigert's room, however, she could hear the murmur of low voices, and she stopped.

"I didn't know you were going to get involved in something as stupid as this," Mrs. Reigert was saying. "Have you lost your mind? How do you expect to hide what you're doing?" Her voice had lost its soft, syrupy quality.

"It *isn't* stupid," Mark insisted. "Maybe a little dangerous, but look at the reward—thousands of . . . And it was just an unlucky break that the fence went down. . . ." He lowered his voice and the rest of the words faded into an inaudible jumble.

"Yes." Mrs. Reigert's voice was hardly any clearer. "But smuggling . . . such high risk . . . if the old man ever finds out . . ." The words began to fade away again, so Nancy put her ear to the door. What kind of illegal activity was Mark involved in? Was it connected to the kidnapping or was it something completely different?

Mrs. Reigert was still talking and Nancy, engrossed, pressed her ear harder against the door, hoping to be able to make out what she was saying.

After a few moments she could hear Mark's voice. It had grown much louder. ". . . don't care *what* you think. You don't have any hold over me. You can't tell me what to do!" Nancy heard him step toward the door and she jumped back.

But it was too late. Mark, on his way out of the room, had yanked the door open. Nancy had been caught!

Chapter

Ten

FOR A SECOND Mark just stared at Nancy. Then he smiled sarcastically. "Well, if it isn't the lovely Miss Driscoll, ghostwriter extraordinaire." With a slight bow, he held the door open wider. "Come right in, please, Miss Driscoll. We're eager to talk to you."

Nancy looked around. The hall was deserted. "Oh, thank you," she said uneasily, "but I—"

"This isn't an invitation, it's an order," Mark snapped. "I said, *come in!*" He grabbed her arm and pulled her into the room, firmly shutting the door behind them.

Mrs. Reigert edged toward them, twisting her

hands. "How much do you suppose she heard, Mark?"

"Shut up, Jonelle," Mark growled. "It's not a question of what she heard, it's a question of why she was listening."

Mark's fingers tightened around Nancy's arm. "All right, my friend," he said, his face close to hers. "I want some answers, and I want them now. Just what brings you to Casa del Alamo, and why are you snooping around outside my mother's door, listening to a private conversation?"

Nancy swallowed, thinking fast. Her best defense, she decided, was to play the injured innocent. "But I *wasn't* snooping," she said tearfully, trying to pull her arm away. "And I wish you'd let go of my arm. You're hurting me!"

"You'd better let her go," Mrs. Reigert said with a worried frown.

Reluctantly, Mark relaxed his fingers. "I still want to know why you were eavesdropping," he said. "And who *are* you anyway?"

Nancy pulled herself up straighter. "I was only walking by," she said. "I heard voices, and I thought I heard somebody say my name. So I stopped. That's when you opened the door and yelled at me."

She began to whimper. "I'm not *used* to being yelled at. And I don't know why you tried to hurt me. I wasn't doing anything." A big tear collected at the corner of each of her eyes and rolled down her cheeks.

Nancy saw that her tears were confusing Mark, but he wasn't ready to back off.

"I don't care what you say. I know you were eavesdropping," he insisted angrily.

Mrs. Reigert handed Nancy a tissue from the silver box on her dressing table. "Sometimes Mark is a little rash, Nancy," she said soothingly, putting her arm around Nancy's shoulders. "Please understand. He's under a great deal of pressure right now. And after all, we *don't* know who you are. How can we trust you?"

Nancy began to cry harder. "That's just the problem," she said, sobbing. "It's so hard to do a good job when nobody will cooperate. Mr. Reigert wants me to get background information about his family, but nobody will talk to me. . . ."

"I know, dear," Mrs. Reigert said sympathetically, leading Nancy to the door. "But you're an outsider and you're asking all sorts of personal questions. It's not easy for *us* either."

"Jonelle, you're letting her get away with—" Mark broke out furiously.

"Shut up, Mark," Mrs. Reigert commanded in an icy tone. "Now, dear," she said, pushing Nancy's hair back from her eyes, "you go on to your room and lie down for a little while. You don't want your eyes all puffy for the party, do you?"

Nancy shook her head. "And I wasn't eavesdropping," she protested plaintively. She threw an injured glance at Mark. "No matter what he says."

"I know, I know," Mrs. Reigert said soothingly. "Now run along." She gave Nancy a little push into the hall and shut the door behind her.

Nancy wiped her tears away. Mrs. Reigert had fallen for her ploy! She returned quickly to her room to sort out what she had heard. Mrs. Reigert had accused Mark of smuggling. But what could he be smuggling, out here in this wild, deserted land? Whatever his dirty work, was it connected to the scheme to take half a million dollars in ransom money from Mr. Reigert?

After Mr. Reigert woke up, Nancy talked with him a few minutes to let him know that Sam Lawson was coming later that night with the money. They would have talked longer, but Gene came in on ranch business, so she left.

Nancy spent the rest of the afternoon trying to get through to Ned, but nobody was answering the phone. Anyway, it would soon be time for the party, which was going to be elaborate. The house was filled with vases of flowers and the gardens decorated with colorful Mexican lanterns and piñatas. A bar was set up, and the members of the mariachi band began to tune up in the hall. By seven the first guests had arrived and the party had begun.

Nancy had packed only two dresses, so she

didn't have much difficulty deciding what to wear to the party. She chose a white sleeveless dress with a low neck and a full skirt.

The guests, most of them from nearby ranches and the town of Rio Hondo, seemed to be having a good time as she wandered among them. They were standing in little knots, sampling the elaborate hors d'oeuvres that had been arranged on trays. Long tables had been set up on the candlelit patio, and they were now loaded with Mexican dishes, most of them hot and spicy. The members of the band wandered through the house and the gardens in their fringed outfits, playing their instruments.

After a while Nancy went in search of the Reigerts. She found Mrs. Reigert on the patio, wearing a daringly cut red dress and a glittering diamond necklace. She was at the center of a circle of admiring men. Mr. Reigert was inside, sitting in a corner, talking to several old friends. He smiled at Nancy when she approached him, but she thought that his smile seemed a little forced and weak. He introduced her quickly and then stood up.

"I know it's early," he said to the others, "but I've been a little under the weather lately. Please excuse me. I—I think I'll go to my room. I—" His face turned slightly gray and he clutched at his stomach.

"Mr. Reigert," Nancy said worriedly, "are you all right?"

"Of course I'm all right," he replied. His words seemed somewhat slurred. "I'm just tired. And this stomach of mine is kicking up again. Can't get that taste of garlic out of my—" He doubled over suddenly.

Gene appeared at Nancy's elbow. "Is he having another attack?" he asked softly.

Nancy nodded. She put one arm around Mr. Reigert's waist. "Can you take the other side?" she asked Gene. "I think we'd better get him to bed."

"Thank you," Mr. Reigert said as they helped him down the hall and into his room. "I'll be better in a few minutes." He lay back on the bed, taking a deep breath. Gene stood watching for a moment, and then left. When he had gone, Nancy pulled a chair up to the edge of the bed and sat down.

"Mr. Reigert," she said at last, "did it ever occur to you that somebody might be poisoning you?"

Chapter

Eleven

Mr. Reigert's eyes opened wide and he looked up at her. "Poisoning me?" he asked. "You've got to be joking."

"No, I'm serious," Nancy said. "Deadly serious. We can't be sure, of course, unless you consent to see a doctor and have some tests. But these attacks are beginning to look very suspicious to me. So does the funny taste that you've complained of. It's possible that someone might be tampering with your food, isn't it?"

"I suppose it is," Mr. Reigert said slowly. "I hadn't thought about it, but I suppose it is."

"And since you're known to distrust doctors, poisoning you would be quite easy, wouldn't it?"

Nancy persisted. "Especially if the poison is cumulative, administered in small doses at first, so that it appears to everyone that you're suffering from some sort of chronic gastrointestinal condition. How long have you been having these attacks?"

Mr. Reigert thought. "A couple of months," he replied. "No longer than that. But who would want to poison me? And why?"

"Who stands to inherit your estate?" Nancy asked in return. "That's always the first question."

"My wife, of course," Mr. Reigert said unhappily. "That is, unless you find my daughter, in which case *she'll* inherit everything." He stared at Nancy. "You don't think that my wife would try to—"

"I don't think anything," Nancy said matter-of-factly. "I'm not making accusations. I just don't want to ignore any of the possibilities, that's all. But I think it would be a very good idea for you to let a doctor examine you right away, so that we can learn what the cause of these attacks is. When we know more, we may be able to rule out poisoning."

Mr. Reigert sighed. "Well, I—"

But he didn't get to finish his sentence. "Darling!" Mrs. Reigert burst into the room, followed by Mark. "I heard you were taken sick again, and I came as soon as I could get away from that awful Mrs. Farraday. She just kept on talking and talking." Mrs. Reigert saw Nancy sitting beside the bed and her face hardened. "What are *you* doing here?" she demanded angrily.

"Nancy helped me to my room," Mr. Reigert said. His voice was cold. "I looked around for you, but you were busy with your admirers." He turned his face away from her. "Don't worry, Jonelle, I won't interfere with your party or your conversation with Mrs. Farraday—or anyone else, for that matter. I don't want to talk to you. Just go away and leave me alone."

"Well!" Mrs. Reigert said, looking offended. "From the tone of your voice, you don't appear to be *too* sick." She whirled around and started out the door. "Come on, Mark. We're obviously not needed here. Nancy Driscoll has everything very well in hand!"

Mark looked back hesitantly. "Are you sure we shouldn't stick around to—?"

"I said, come on, Mark!" Mark turned and followed Mrs. Reigert.

After they had gone, Mr. Reigert lay still for a while, his eyes closed. Then he opened them and said, "You're right, Nancy. The only way to find out whether poison is involved is for me to see a doctor. I'll make an appointment with that young fellow in Rio Hondo tomorrow." He grimaced. "I don't like it, but I'll do it."

Nancy grinned. "I'm glad," she said. If he wasn't being poisoned, at least Mr. Reigert could be treated for his stomach ailment. She glanced down at her watch. "Why don't you nap for a little while? Mr. Lawson isn't due to arrive with the money for a couple of hours."

Mr. Reigert nodded, and Nancy sat beside his bed while he fell into a regular sleep, breathing normally. As she watched him, she reviewed the central questions of the case.

There were the ransom notes, of course, although she still couldn't be sure there had been an actual kidnapping. There were the attempts on *her* life. And now there were what might be attempts on Mr. Reigert's life. And in the background was that puzzling business of the strange animals, first the deer, then the kangaroo. But how were all these different things tied together?

Nancy looked at her watch. It was nearly eleven o'clock. In a few minutes it would be time to go to her room and change into jeans and a shirt, and then saddle up the horses so she could meet Mr. Lawson.

There was a tentative knock on the door and it opened slightly. "Miss Driscoll?" a soft, hesitant voice asked.

Nancy whirled around. Angela was standing at the door. She looked worried, her dark eyes intense.

"How is the senor?" she asked. "I heard that he was taken ill again at the party. Will he be all right?"

"He's asleep now," Nancy said gently. "He's feeling much better. And he's agreed to see a doctor tomorrow."

Angela closed her eyes and sagged in relief against the door frame. *"Gracias a Dios,"* she murmured. "Thank God."

Nancy stared at her, puzzled. Then she took the girl by the arm and pulled her out into the hall, shutting the door behind them. "Angela," she said urgently, "I am Mr. Reigert's friend. I want to be your friend too. But I *must* know why you are so concerned about Mr. Reigert. You've got to tell me."

Angela stepped backward. "I cannot tell you," she said, pulling herself up straight.

"Why not?" asked Nancy. "I have the feeling that you want to help Mr. Reigert, just as I do. Perhaps, working together, we *can* help him."

For a moment, Nancy had the feeling that Angela was on the brink of telling her something very important, something that might break the case wide open. Was it possible that she had some inside information about the kidnapping, or about Mr. Reigert's mysterious illness?

"I cannot," Angela said with a quiet dignity, her dark eyes intent on Nancy's face. "But I thank you, Nancy Driscoll, for your kind regard for Senor Reigert. You are indeed his friend, in a place where he is surrounded by those who wish him harm."

And with that surprising remark she walked away.

* * *

It was a few minutes before midnight when Nancy arrived on horseback at the arched gateway to Casa del Alamo, the reins of a spare horse tied to the saddle of her palomino. Mr. Lawson stepped out of his car, which he had hidden in a clump of trees out of sight of the main road. He was carrying a small green duffel bag.

"Is that the money?" Nancy asked.

"It's the money," Mr. Lawson replied shortly, handing it to Nancy. "I've been involved in some strange transactions in my time," he added. "But this one takes the cake."

Nancy smiled in spite of herself as Mr. Lawson mounted the other horse. Then they rode in silence down the deserted road, its dust turned to silver by the light of the full moon.

When they reached the house, they tied the horses in the dark shadows of a grove of tall pecan trees and walked quietly through the garden. It was nearly twelve-thirty, and the party was over. The house was silent and dark, except for a light in the kitchen. Mrs. Arguello or Angela must still be cleaning up, Nancy thought.

Their path led beside the house, under the closed casement windows of the bedrooms along the hall, and Nancy motioned for Mr. Lawson to be very quiet. Stealthily and with great caution, they crept along.

At one point, Nancy turned quickly, sure that she had heard something behind them, perhaps the scraping sound of a casement window swinging open. But it must have been her imagination, for the windows were all closed tightly and the moon-lit gardens seemed to be deserted. Still, Nancy breathed a quiet sigh of relief when they reached the side door of the house and stepped inside.

Mr. Reigert was awake and waiting for them, dressed in robe and pajamas, with the curtains tightly drawn in his bedroom. Nancy shut the door as soon as Mr. Lawson had stepped into the room.

"You've brought the money, Sam?" Mr. Reigert asked, his voice very low.

"I've brought it, Bob," Mr. Lawson answered testily. "But I was tempted to bring the sheriff too. If Billy McPhee weren't such a bad joke of a sheriff, I would have for certain."

He shook his head. "I tell you, Bob, I *still* don't understand a bit of this. I know you can't tell me why you need the money, but are you in some kind of trouble?"

Mr. Reigert frowned. "No questions, Sam," he said. "I can't tell you any more than I told you on the phone. Maybe later, but not now. All I want now is the money. After all, it *is* my money."

"Well, here it is, blast it," Mr. Lawson replied. He put the duffel bag on the bed and unzipped it. "I certainly hope you've got someplace safe to stow all this cash. A half million dollars is too much to leave lying loose around the house."

"How's this?" Mr. Reigert crossed the room to the paneled wall beside the window and pressed a hidden button. A portion of the wall swung outward, revealing a small safe. "Just installed last year," he said. "The money should be as safe here as it is in your bank." He grinned, "Maybe safer."

"I hope so, for your sake." Mr. Lawson watched while Mr. Reigert counted the money, put it in the safe, and locked it. When the paneling swung back into place, it was so well hidden that Nancy couldn't even see where the opening had been.

Mr. Lawson looked at Mr. Reigert. "That withdrawal wipes you out, you know, Bob," he observed thoughtfully. "The money in that safe represents all your liquid assets. At least, all that you've been keeping in *my* bank."

"I know," Mr. Reigert replied.

"Well, I guess you understand what you're doing then," Mr. Lawson said. There was a puzzled look on his face, and he put his hand on Mr. Reigert's arm. "Listen, Bob, you look exhausted. Are you sure you're all right?"

Mr. Reigert passed his hand over his eyes. "It's been a rough day," he admitted wearily. "But I'll feel better after I get a good night's sleep." He looked at Nancy. "And Nancy's even talked me into letting that young whippersnapper of a doctor over in Rio Hondo take a look at me."

Mr. Lawson chuckled. "Good for you. But you know the old prescription for a good night's sleep. A glass of warm milk with a hefty shot of whiskey in it." He hesitated. "If you need any help, you know you can call on me. I'll be glad to do whatever I can."

"Thanks, Sam," Mr. Reigert said, going to the door with them. "But you've already helped enough—at least for now."

"Well, then, I'll be getting back to town," Mr. Lawson replied. "Good luck, Bob. Whatever the problem is, I hope you get it solved."

"So do I," Mr. Reigert said fervently. "So do I."

Thirty minutes later, Nancy was saying goodbye to the banker beside his car.

"I don't know who you are, Nancy Driscoll," Mr. Lawson said, "but it's obvious that Bob Reigert trusts you. And I guess that's good enough for me. There aren't very many people in the world whom Bob thinks he can trust." He got into his car. "Keep an eye on him and call me if you need me."

"I will," Nancy said. "And thanks." She watched Mr. Lawson back the car onto the road and drive off. When the sound of the motor had faded away, Nancy turned and rode slowly down the lane, the riderless horse trotting beside her. On either side, the land fell away, still and lovely under the silver moon.

But Nancy hardly saw the moonlight or the dancing shadows that were stirred into life by the gentle midnight breeze. She was thinking about the next day. If Mr. Reigert received instructions from the kidnappers, she would insist on seeing the birthmark to prove that the girl really *was* Catarina.

While they were waiting for the kidnappers to make contact, Mr. Reigert could go to the doctor to see what could be discovered about his stomach-aches. Until the truth was known, she would have to caution him to eat and drink only food that they could prove was not poisoned. And the next day she would have to contact Ned in Dallas. Maybe, by that time, he would have been able to learn something about Mrs. Reigert's mysterious background.

Nancy was so involved in her planning that she was only vaguely aware of the rumbling sound that seemed to rise up out of the road, breaking the stillness of the night. When she finally heard it, she looked up. Just ahead the road curved, and there was nothing in sight, as far as she could see. Still, the rumbling grew louder. The palomino perked up her ears.

"What do you suppose—?" Nancy asked herself out loud. The mare began to prance nervously, and Nancy reined her in.

Then, suddenly, she saw a black shadow bearing down on her. A huge semitrailer, its lights turned off, had rounded the curve just ahead. It was barreling down the road straight at her!

Chapter

Twelve

FOR AN INSTANT Nancy panicked. The huge truck, like a giant, rumbling shadow in the moonlight, was bearing down on her so fast there was hardly time to think. But she recovered her wits, jabbed her heels hard into the flanks of the palomino, lashing her with the reins, and rode her as fast as she could into the dark ditch along the road.

And not a minute too soon. She had barely managed to get the horses off the road when the truck whizzed past her, its lights still out. She stared after it as it rounded another curve, hidden in a cloud of dust that hung silvery in the moonlight long after the truck had completely disappeared.

It had been a large semitrailer with slatted sides. Nancy wasn't sure, but she thought it had looked like a stock truck. What was a stock truck doing out there at night with no lights on? Maybe it had something to do with the bull that Mr. Reigert had bought. But it didn't seem logical that anyone would be delivering a bull so late at night.

The palomino gave a soft, plaintive nicker, as if to remind Nancy that it was time to go back to the stable, so Nancy let the horse have its head as she rode back onto the road. She decided that she would ask Mr. Reigert about the truck in the morning. Perhaps he would have some clue as to what might be going on.

The rest of the ride back to the ranch house was quiet, and Nancy was grateful. She'd had enough excitement for one night. The party, Mr. Reigert's attack of stomach pains, Mr. Lawson's arrival with the money, and the near-miss with the stock truck. It had certainly been an eventful evening!

When Nancy reached the corral, she unsaddled the horses and gave them a quick brushing down. It was nearly two o'clock, and Nancy was bone weary. Not only that, but her cowboy boots were pinching her feet as well.

She went into the house and walked down the hall toward her bedroom, trying not to make any noise. But as she walked past Mr. Reigert's room, she heard what sounded like the casement window banging shut. When she and Mr. Lawson had left, the window had been closed and the heavy draperies pulled together. Mr. Reigert had said he was very tired and was planning to go right back to bed.

Maybe he had opened the window, and it was swinging in the wind. But there was only a slight breeze, hardly enough to slam the window. Perhaps he had just now gotten up and opened the window. If so, Nancy wanted to ask him about the truck. She was eager to start piecing together the strange events of the last few days.

Hesitantly, Nancy knocked at the door. She could hear Mr. Reigert's bed creak as if he had turned over. But if Mr. Reigert were still in bed, who had banged the window? Nancy reached for the knob and found that it turned easily. She stepped into the room.

"Mr. Reigert," she whispered. "It's Nancy. Is everything all right?" She looked toward the window. The breeze was stirring the heavy drapes.

A shapeless mass moved on the bed. "Nancy?" Mr. Reigert sat up. "What are *you* doing here?" he demanded, his voice slurred with sleep.

"I was walking past your door," Nancy explained, "and I heard a noise. It sounded like your window banging shut. So I came in."

"Nonsense." Mr. Reigert leaned over and fumbled to turn on the small bedside lamp. A circle of golden light spilled across the bed, and Nancy noticed an empty glass on the bedside table. It looked as if it had held milk. "That window has been locked all day," he added, reaching for his robe. "And I locked my door before I went to bed! I always do."

"Then why are the drapes blowing?" Nancy stepped toward the window. "The window *is* open!" she reported excitedly. "And your door *was* unlocked!"

"But how?" Mr. Reigert asked blankly. "I was sure . . . The money! Could the money have been—?" He stumbled to the hidden button on the wall and pushed it. The paneling swung out silently, and Mr. Reigert turned the combination lock on the safe door while Nancy watched. After a moment the door opened and Mr. Reigert reached inside.

"Oh, no," he moaned.

"What's the matter?" Nancy asked.

"The money's gone!" Mr. Reigert buried his face in his hands. "It's gone! I can't pay the ransom!"

Nancy pushed Mr. Reigert aside and peered into the safe. It was empty! The money had been stolen!

"What can I do? What can I do?" Mr. Reigert slumped into the chair beside the window, his chin resting on his chest, eyes closed. His face suddenly looked pale and drawn.

Nancy knelt on the floor beside him. "Mr.

Reigert," she said urgently, "are you feeling well enough to talk? I need to ask you some questions."

"I'll be all right in a few minutes," he said, not opening his eyes. "Ask me what you have to."

"What happened after Mr. Lawson and I left this evening? Did you go straight to bed?"

Mr. Reigert put his hand to his forehead and began to rub his eyes. "I—I went to the kitchen," he said slowly. "To get a glass of milk. I put some whiskey into it to help me sleep. Then I came back into the room, locked the door, and went to bed."

"Did you see anyone or talk to anyone?"

"Only Mrs. Reigert," Mr. Reigert responded. "She came into the kitchen just as I was leaving."

"Did you talk with her?"

"She asked me what I was doing up so late, and how I was feeling. I told her I was getting something to help me sleep and that I felt fine. That's all we said." He laughed bitterly. "I suppose you've gathered that we don't have much to say to each other."

"And you didn't see anyone else?" Nancy persisted.

Mr. Reigert shook his head, looking very old and weary. "I came back to my room, locked the door, drank the milk, and went to bed." He looked up suddenly. "But if the door was locked, how did *you* get in?"

"Someone must have come in before I did," Nancy replied. "Who else has a key to your room?

More important, who else knows the combination to the safe? Whoever took the money probably came in through the door, opened the safe, and then decided to go out by the window to avoid being seen in the hallway."

"But who?"

"Who knows about the safe?"

"It wasn't exactly a secret," Mr. Reigert said. He rested his head in his hand. "I suppose the whole household knew that I was having it built. But the combination—that's a secret. Nobody knows it but me."

"Is it written down anywhere?"

"Yes. I keep a copy in . . ." His voice trailed off, and he looked up at Nancy, his eyes watery. "There was a copy of the combination in the drawer where the wedding picture was," he said. "It's still there," he added.

"But whoever took the wedding picture could have copied the combination to the safe at the same time," Nancy replied, standing up.

Mr. Reigert nodded. "Where are you going?"

Nancy went to the bedside table and turned out the light. She reached into her shirt pocket for the small flashlight. "To look for clues," she said.

The light out, she pulled open the draperies. The window had swung against the outside wall, and Nancy shone her light first on the windowsill and then on the ground beneath. The sill yielded nothing, but under the window, in the soft earth of the flowerbed, she saw the smudged print of a heel. Being careful not to disturb anything, Nancy climbed out to look more closely at the print.

"Do you see anything?" Mr. Reigert whispered, leaning out the window.

"Not a thing," Nancy reported. And then something glinted in the beam of her flashlight. She reached over and picked it up. "Except this," she said.

"What is it?" Mr. Reigert asked.

"It's a button," Nancy replied. "A silver button with the Reigert brand! Exactly like the buttons on the shirt that Mrs. Reigert was wearing the day I arrived!"

Chapter

Thirteen

A BUTTON?" MR. Reigert exclaimed.

"The thief probably caught a shirtsleeve on the casement window," Nancy said, climbing back into the room and closing the drapes. She put the button on the bedside table and turned on the light, and they both bent over to examine it.

"It looks like a button from Mrs. Reigert's shirt, doesn't it?" Nancy asked.

"I don't know," Mr. Reigert replied. "A couple of years ago I had a number of these silver buttons made up as Christmas presents for the staff."

"So *everyone* was given some of the buttons?" Nancy asked.

"Everyone," Mr. Reigert replied evenly. "Mrs. Arguello, Gene, Joe Bob, even the cowboys. When Mrs. Reigert and I were married, she admired the buttons, so I gave her several sets, as well."

"Well," said Nancy, "right now I suggest that we try to get some sleep. It's very late. And tomorrow morning we need to contact the police and let them know about the theft."

Mr. Reigert's tired blue eyes flashed. "Let Billy McPhee know that somebody walked out of Casa del Alamo with half a million dollars? Not on your life," he said emphatically.

"Mr. Reigert," Nancy replied, "I am a responsible private detective. I can't be a party to a large theft like this without calling in the proper authorities and—"

"And I'm telling you that you can forget about calling in the law," Mr. Reigert said stubbornly. "I won't have it.

"Anyway," he added, "the last note said that the kidnappers would be contacting us tomorrow or the next day. The notes have all been hand delivered, so the kidnappers must be around here somewhere or have accomplices here. That sorry excuse for a sheriff is about as subtle as a bulldozer. If he starts nosing around, questioning everybody about the missing money, the kidnappers might get wind of it. And then where would we be?"

He dropped down on the edge of the bed,

looking worn and defeated. "They might just kill my daughter."

"But we don't *know* that the girl on the tape is Catarina," Nancy pointed out. "We're not sure whether we have a case of kidnapping on our hands, or a simple case of blackmail."

She thought for a moment. "But in either event," she conceded, "I suppose it wouldn't help us to call in the police just yet. We have to convince the extortionists that we're not going to pay up unless they show us evidence that the girl they have is *really* Catarina."

"The birthmark," Mr. Reigert said, lying down on the bed. He closed his eyes.

"Yes, the birthmark," Nancy repeated. She was bending over to switch off the light when she suddenly remembered what had happened earlier that evening. She straightened up. "Mr. Reigert," she asked, "why would a semitrailer truck be running down the road out of the ranch in the middle of the night with its lights off?"

"A semi?" Mr. Reigert asked blurrily. "At night? You must be mistaken. We don't run trucks on this ranch at night. . . ." His voice was trailing off. "Especially without lights."

"No," Nancy said firmly. "I'm not mistaken. I didn't see it until it was almost too late. It nearly ran me down. What do you think—?"

But Nancy's question was interrupted by a gentle snore. Mr. Reigert had fallen asleep.

* * *

Nancy wasn't as fortunate as Mr. Reigert. She went to bed as soon as she got back to her room, but it was over an hour before she fell asleep. She longed to talk to Ned, even though she knew it was far too late to call him. She sighed.

The missing money had added another piece to an already jumbled puzzle. The thief must have known that the money was in the safe, but how? Had someone been expecting the delivery, or had someone seen her and Mr. Lawson as they came to the house?

She remembered the moment in the garden when she thought she had heard a window opening. The thief might have looked out of one of the bedrooms, seen the two of them, and recognized the banker. Whoever had taken the money also had to have a key to Mr. Reigert's room and the combination to the safe.

Nancy pulled the pillow over her head. Right then, there was such a confusion of possible crimes and potential criminals that it seemed impossible to unravel them.

Breakfast the next morning was gloomy and silent. Mr. Reigert appeared, looking pale and wan. He ate nothing, just poured himself a cup of coffee, which he took back to his room. No one else spoke, and Nancy finished eating as quickly as possible. After excusing herself, she left the table and followed Mr. Reigert to his room.

"How about seeing that doctor today?" she asked.

"I'll call for an appointment as soon as they open," he told her. "I know he'll make room to see me later this afternoon. He's been trying to get me in there for months." He made a face. "I tell you, though, I'm not looking forward to it."

"I understand," Nancy replied. "But it will help us clear up one mystery anyway. As far as the others are concerned . . ." She glanced at her watch. She wanted to try calling Ned again. But when she went back to her room to make the call, there was no answer. Apparently, Ned had gone out *very* early.

Frustrated, Nancy hung up and started down the hall. But she was stopped by Gene Newsom, who was just coming out of Mr. Reigert's office.

"There's a phone call for you, Nancy," Gene said. "You can take it in there." He gestured toward the office.

"A phone call?" Nancy asked. Ned, Hannah Gruen, and her father were the only people who knew the phone number, and none of them would call her unless it was an emergency.

Nancy rushed into the empty office and picked up the phone. "This is Nancy—Driscoll," she said, remembering to use her pseudonym at the last moment.

"This is a friend," a muffled voice on the other end of the line answered. "I have the information you need for Mr. Reigert."

115

"You have what?" Nancy asked in surprise. She held the receiver closer to her ear and began to stall for time. She *had* to hear that voice again. Maybe she could identify it. "Who is this?" she asked. "What kind of information are you talking about?"

"It doesn't matter who I am," the voice said. It was so low and so distorted that Nancy couldn't even tell whether it belonged to a man or a woman, although she thought she detected the hint of an accent. "In order to find out what kind of information I have, meet me in the wine cellar in thirty minutes." There was a sudden click, then the line went dead.

Nancy sat staring at the phone. She knew she had to meet the mysterious caller, whoever he—or she—was. But she had learned at least one lesson from the disastrous adventure in the stable a few nights before. She wasn't going to be a sitting duck again. She was going to arrive before the caller did and watch from a hidden position. This time, the advantage of surprise would be on *her* side.

The wine cellar was reached through an outside door at the back of the house that led directly onto a dark flight of stairs. Watching to be sure that she wasn't seen, Nancy crept outside and opened the door. The rough-timbered stairs slanted down steeply. Nancy closed the heavy oak door behind her and felt around for the light switch. She was enveloped by a cool darkness. But then she clicked the light on and the darkness disappeared.

Nancy looked down. The light, a green-shaded bulb at the foot of the stairs, cast a small circle of pale light in the sooty darkness. Holding her breath, Nancy gingerly went down the stairs. The cellar was small, no more than fifteen feet square, hewn in the limestone rock on which the ranch house had been built. Wine racks had been built along two walls, and dusty bottles filled them from floor to ceiling.

Carefully Nancy looked around, taking extra time to search the dark space beneath the stairs, where several wooden boxes were stacked. The cellar was obviously empty, and she let out a little sigh. So far, so good. Whoever her informant was, and whatever the motive, she had gotten there ahead of him—or her.

She glanced up at the light, thinking. Then she felt around the wall behind the stairs. Yes, there *was* another switch there. Pulling her small pocketknife out of the pocket of her jeans, Nancy hurried up the stairs and removed the cover of the switchplate. Then, holding her flashlight in her teeth, she unscrewed the switch itself and yanked the wires loose. The light went out.

Guiding herself down the stairs with the flashlight, Nancy flicked the other switch. The light came on. Good! She could control it from under the stairs. But it couldn't be controlled from upstairs. Now all she had to do was hide herself and get ready.

The minutes seemed to tick by interminably for

Nancy as she crouched under the stairs. She looked at her watch again. It was ten minutes before the appointed hour. Surely the caller would be along soon.

Finally, on the landing above her, Nancy heard someone fumbling with the door handle. A puddle of light cascaded down the stairs and then disappeared as the door was shut. Nancy could hear the faint whispering of a muffled consultation, as someone seemed to be feeling for the disabled light switch. So there were two people!

There was more muttered consultation. Then an unidentifiable voice whispered, "Another switch at the bottom of the stairs." And footsteps began to descend the creaking stairs over Nancy's head.

Holding her breath, Nancy waited until the first pair of footsteps reached the bottom. Then she flicked the switch on the wall beside her.

The bulb cast its circle of light on the dirt floor of the cellar, and Nancy gasped as the figure was revealed.

Chapter

Fourteen

Angela!" Nancy exclaimed, stepping out of her hiding place. "So *you* were the one who telephoned me! I thought the call came from somewhere outside the ranch."

Angela turned, her gaze steady on Nancy. "Yes, it *was* I who telephoned you," she said in a low voice. "I used the house line to call the office line." Her dark eyes were shadowed and a mysterious smile played on her lips. She had an almost aristocratic look. "But my name is not Angela."

"Not Angela?" Nancy asked, staring at her.

Suddenly it all clicked. Angela's age and proud appearance, her obvious concern for Mr. Reigert's health, her interest in his family affairs—

Angela the housemaid was Mr. Reigert's long-lost daughter!

"Catarina," Nancy said softly. "You are Catarina Reigert."

Suddenly Mrs. Arguello stepped off the stairs and into the light. "*Sí,*" she said. "You are right, Nancy Driscoll. Angela's true name is Catarina Reigert."

Nancy's mind raced through the facts of the case as she knew them so far. If Angela was Catarina Reigert, then the girl in the videotape was an impostor. And the kidnapping itself was a hoax, probably arranged for the sole purpose of tricking Mr. Reigert into withdrawing his savings and putting it where it could be easily stolen!

Then Nancy's sense of caution brought another idea to her mind. Perhaps *this* girl in front of her was the impostor—and the girl in the tape was the real Catarina Reigert! There was only one way to tell, and that was the birthmark.

Nancy turned to Mrs. Arguello. "I would like to see proof of this girl's identity," she said. "How can you prove that Angela is who she claims to be?"

"Read this," Mrs. Arguello said, thrusting a rolled-up piece of paper toward Nancy. "This will tell you what you want to know."

Nancy held the paper up so that the light fell on it. It was a birth certificate, documenting the birth of Catarina Reigert to Robert and Isabel Reigert, seventeen years before.

"But this paper doesn't tell me anything about Catarina herself or whether *this* young woman is Catarina," Nancy objected. "What proof can you give me that the girl who calls herself Angela is the same girl whose birth is documented in this paper?"

"Proof?" Angela asked, stepping closer to Nancy. "You want proof?" She held out her right foot. "This is the birthmark of Catarina Reigert," she said triumphantly. "My father is sure to remember it, for I am told that my mother had a similar mark in the same place."

Nancy stared at the girl's right ankle. There it was, the strawberry-shaped mark that Mr. Reigert had described earlier. There could be no doubt about it. Angela *was* Catarina Reigert! The kidnapping had been a hoax!

Nancy took Catarina's hand. She decided she would keep the kidnapping to herself, since it seemed unlikely that Catarina and Mrs. Arguello knew anything about it.

"I am sure that your father will be very glad to know who you are, Catarina," she said softly. She turned to Mrs. Arguello. "But how is it that Catarina came to be here, at Casa del Alamo? Why did she disguise herself as a housemaid? Why hasn't she revealed her identity to her father? And why have you chosen to tell *me,* and not to tell him?"

Mrs. Arguello smiled. "Questions, questions, so many questions," she said, her black eyes softer than Nancy had seen them. "But I will be glad to answer them as best I can, if you will be kind enough to listen. And then we must ask for your help, to save Senor Reigert's life."

"So he *is* being poisoned," Nancy exclaimed. "And you know who's behind it!"

"*Sí.*" The old woman nodded. "We know. But first I must tell you the story of Isabel and Catarina Reigert, and then the rest will make sense to you." She pulled a wooden box into the light, sat down on it, and began to talk.

"I came here from Mexico with Isabel when she came to marry Senor Reigert." A smile came into her eyes. "I was nursemaid to Catarina, and after the terrible quarrel I was supposed to accompany Isabel and Catarina back to Mexico. But I was ill and could not travel—and then there was the plane crash, and when I learned of the deaths, I stayed on with Senor Reigert."

She sighed and shifted position. "But the plane crash that killed Isabel and the pilot," she said, "did not kill Catarina. The crash occurred as the plane was landing on the airstrip on the estate of Isabel's parents, a coffee plantation high in the mountains of Mexico. The little girl was pulled from the wreckage, only slightly injured, and taken to her grandparents."

She looked up at Nancy. "As you guessed earlier, Isabel's mother and father had never approved of her marriage. . . ."

"So they decided to keep the little girl," Nancy

guessed, "and let her father believe that she had died in the crash that killed his wife!"

"Just so." Mrs. Arguello nodded. "Because they loved Isabel and mourned her death, they wished to raise her daughter. They did not want her to return to what they believed would be a life of poverty and unhappiness with her father in Texas."

"It truly was not that they hated him so, even though they did not approve of the marriage," Catarina interjected softly. She sat down on the step and put her chin in her hands. "It was just that they loved me, and so they kept me and told him that I was dead, as my mother was dead."

"And you?" Nancy asked. "What did they tell you?"

Catarina's soft brown eyes were sad. "They told me that my father was dead, too, just as my mother. And they gave me a home and made me in every way their beloved daughter."

"But why did you decide to return to Texas?" Nancy prompted. "How did you find out that your father was alive?"

Catarina nodded at Mrs. Arguello. "It was she," she said. "Senora Arguello came to my grandparents' home and told me about my father. When I learned of him, I wished to be with him, and after a while I came to Texas with her."

Mrs. Arguello smiled. "Catarina makes it sound easy. But it was not easy."

"I suppose that Catarina's grandparents didn't want to let her leave."

"No, they did not want her to go," the old woman said sadly. "It is this way. A few months ago I learned from my cousin Jorge that he thought Catarina was alive and living with her grandparents, so I traveled to Mexico to see for myself, and I stayed for a time on the plantation.

"At last I spoke to Catarina and told her about her father, that he was alive and that he loved her." Her black eyes flashed in the age-seamed face. "And when she heard, she wished to return with me to visit her father.

"But her grandparents did not wish her to go away from them. They had already made a plan, you see, for their granddaughter to marry their friend's oldest son and unite their two estates."

A sad smile played around Catarina's lips. "They did not consult me in the matter of this marriage," she said. "It is the old way, you see, where the family decides upon the husband, no matter what the desires of the couple. And even after I told them I could not love the man they had chosen for my husband, they were still determined that we should marry. It was arranged, in spite of my wishes, and against all my protests.

"And so when Senora Arguello left to return to the United States, I left with her, late one night, when all were asleep." She smiled proudly. "I could travel easily across the border, for my birth certificate proves that I am an American citizen!"

"I understand," Nancy said, her heart full of sympathy for the young woman who had narrowly escaped marriage to a man she didn't love. "But why didn't you reveal yourself to your father when you arrived at Casa del Alamo?"

"I meant to," Catarina said. Her smile became a little crooked. "But I learned that my father had unexpectedly taken a new wife, who had a son.

"At first they all seemed very happy together, and the time did not seem right for my father to learn that he had a daughter, as well as a new son. And then after a while, I began to worry that his new wife and her son did not have a real love for him, and I thought it best to wait a little while longer."

"So you watched."

"Yes. I waited and I watched." Catarina's words were measured. "And I learned that my father was becoming very unhappy with his new wife. I learned that she did not love her husband and that her son wished him dead."

"Wished him dead!" Nancy exclaimed. "So *Mark* has been poisoning Mr. Reigert?"

"*Sí,*" Mrs. Arguello replied. She stood up and began to pace back and forth. "That is why we have come to talk to you. The senor is in very great danger and must be warned. We believe that he will accept the truth about this poisoning if it comes from you."

"And what *is* the truth?" Nancy asked, looking at them closely. "What have you seen?"

Catarina clenched her hands into fists at her sides. "Last night, during the party, I saw Mark put something on the dinner plate that Senora Arguello had prepared for my father. It was a white powder. At first I did not know what he was doing, but when my father was taken ill after eating, I realized that Mark has been causing his stomach attacks."

She took a deep breath. "While Mark was at breakfast this morning, I went to his room and searched it. I found this, hidden behind a picture frame." Gingerly, she held out a small glass bottle that bore an aspirin label. But instead of aspirin tablets, the bottle contained a white powder. The bottle was wrapped in a handkerchief.

"This is what I saw him putting on the food, and it is the same bottle. I am sure that it is poison."

Nancy took the bottle, holding it so as not to disturb any fingerprints. "It *could* be poison," she said thoughtfully. "But we can't be sure until it's tested. The nearest forensics lab must be in—"

But Nancy didn't get to finish her sentence. At that moment the oak door at the top of the stairs swung open and then closed again. Heavy footsteps came down the stairs.

Chapter

Fifteen

NANCY THRUST THE bottle into her shirt pocket and held her breath as the footsteps moved down the steps.

"Well, have you told her yet?" a voice demanded from the shadows. It was Gene Newsom!

"*Sí*," Mrs. Arguello said. "We have told her. Or rather," she added, "the senorita guessed before we could tell her. She has a very good mind, this one."

Gene came into the light. "Were you surprised?" he asked. He put his arm around Catarina's shoulders and looked down at her lovingly. "Don't you think Mr. Reigert will be proud of his beautiful daughter?"

Nancy let out her breath explosively. "So, *you're* involved in this too!" Suddenly she understood—Gene was in love with Catarina!

The laugh lines crinkled at the corners of Gene's eyes. "Before she went to Mexico, Mrs. Arguello took me into her confidence. But I must say, I wasn't expecting her to bring back someone like Catarina." He hugged her tightly. "As soon as she's told her father who she is, I'm going to marry her."

"And this time," Nancy said to Catarina, "I suppose you'll consent."

Catarina laughed warmly. "I consent," she said, "*if* my father agrees."

Gene's grin nearly split his face. "And we're both sure that *he* won't mind," he said. "In fact, he'll probably be even happier than we are, if that's possible." He turned to Nancy. "And now I've got a surprise for you."

"For me?" Nancy asked.

"Yes. There's this guy waiting outside. He says he's a friend of yours. Says he just happened to be passing through and thought he'd stop and say hello."

Nancy's heart jumped up into her mouth. "Is he tall and dark?" she asked.

Gene laughed. "That's him. Says his name is Ned Nickerson."

Nancy took the steps two at a time and threw open the door. Ned was waiting in the yard, and she motioned eagerly for him to come into the cellar. He looked around to be sure that no one was watching, then followed her down the steps, grinning. At the foot of the steps, he put his hands on her shoulders and looked at her carefully.

"You're all in one piece?" he asked worriedly. "You're okay?"

"I'm a hundred percent better right now," Nancy said, unable to take her eyes from his face. "Now that you're here."

Ned looked at Gene and the others. "Is it okay to talk?" he asked.

"It's okay," Nancy assured him. She briefed him on what she had learned from Catarina and Mrs. Arguello.

"And I've got news for you too," Ned said. "Just before I left, my uncle remembered where he had heard the name Jonelle. Turns out that she and Mark were involved in a scam in Houston a couple of years ago. They took a widow for every penny she had, and they got away before they were found out. And what's more, Jonelle and Mark aren't even related!"

"Not related!" Catarina gasped.

"I think their conning days are about to come to an end," Nancy assured her. "What we have to do now is discover what's in this bottle." She turned to Gene. "Where's the nearest forensics lab?"

"In San Antonio, I think," Gene said. "There's a private airport in Rio Hondo, and I have a pilot's license. I could fly the bottle to the lab this afternoon and be back by dinnertime."

"Great!" Nancy replied. She thought for a moment. If what Catarina had found was poison, and if Mark was responsible for the attempts on Mr. Reigert's life, it was very likely that he was the one who had tried to kill Nancy too—deliberately throwing suspicion on Joe Bob. "I suspect that Mark is behind a great many things that have happened since I came to Casa del Alamo," she said.

"Like saddling Bad Guy for you to ride?" Gene asked.

Ned frowned. "And firing the gun at you? That was what worried me most and made me decide to come."

"Right," Nancy said. "And when *that* didn't work, he dressed up in a clown suit and pushed me off the fence into the pen at the rodeo."

Gene's face turned red with embarrassment. "I wonder what you thought of me that night," he said. "I didn't jump into the pen after you because —well, because I'm bull-shy."

"Bull-shy?"

Catarina stroked his arm. "Gene was thrown last year at the rodeo. He still has trouble getting close to bulls."

Nancy laughed. "I *did* wonder about it," she admitted. "In fact, for a little while you were one of my suspects." She turned to Ned. "Mark was probably the one who smacked me on the head in the stable that night. I thought it was Joe Bob, but he had just put on Joe Bob's coat to make me suspect him."

"So *that's* why you were suspicious of Joe Bob," Gene said thoughtfully. He looked at Nancy, his eyes narrowing. "Just who *are* you, Nancy Driscoll? And what are you doing here?"

Ned chuckled. "Don't you think it's time you told them, Nancy?"

Nancy looked from one to the other. It probably was time to let them in on the deception, now that she was certain they didn't have anything to do with the kidnapping. They might even know something that would help her.

"The truth is," Nancy said, "that I'm a private detective. My name is Nancy Drew."

"A private detective!" Catarina turned pale.

"Mr. Reigert contacted me because he had received a ransom note from someone who claimed to have kidnapped his daughter," Nancy said.

"Ransom notes!" Gene exclaimed.

Catarina laughed. "But that's ridiculous! I'm right here! There's no kidnapping!"

"That's right," Ned said. "But Mr. Reigert couldn't have known that. As far as he knew, his daughter really *was* being held captive."

"Yes," Nancy agreed. "In fact," she added, "he received some interesting evidence along with the

131

notes. A piece of cloth that he recognized as a fragment of the dress Catarina was wearing the day she and her mother left, and a little shoe with a silver bell tied to the lace."

"My shoe!" Catarina wailed. "And a piece of my dress! Someone must have stolen them from the attic, from the box where I put them!"

"The box?" Nancy asked. "You mean, those things belonged to *you?*"

"Yes. I brought some mementos here from Mexico. Perhaps it was sentimental, but I put them in an old box in the attic, where some of my mother's things were stored. It seemed to me that they all belonged together."

"So it's possible," Ned said thoughtfully, "that someone opened the box and found the cloth and the shoes. But how would that person know they belonged to you?"

"Easily," Nancy said. She told the others about the article and picture that had appeared in the Rio Hondo paper after the crash. "It's one of the photographs on the videotape!" she added.

"The videotape?" Gene asked, shaking his head. "What videotape?"

"In addition to the ransom notes, Mr. Reigert received a videotape. It showed a girl claiming to be Catarina, bound to a chair. It also showed two photographs, the one from the newspaper and another taken on the Reigerts' wedding day. Your father says it was stolen from his room."

"He is right," Mrs. Arguello said, regarding Nancy calmly. "I know who took it."

Nancy nodded. "It was Mrs. Reigert, wasn't it?"

"*Sí.* I met her in the hall, coming out of the room with the photograph. She hid it behind her back, but I knew what it was because I had seen it many times before."

"So Mrs. Reigert is in on this phony kidnapping plot?" Ned asked. "But what did she hope to get out of it? I mean, she didn't really have the girl."

"Obviously," Nancy answered, "she hoped to get the ransom money. Half a million dollars in cash. That kind of immediate payoff would be much better than a large inheritance at some indefinite time in the future, wouldn't you say?"

Gene whistled and Catarina's eyes widened. Even the impassive Mrs. Arguello looked startled.

"It must have been Mrs. Reigert," Nancy continued, "who found the mementos in the box in the attic—perhaps quite by accident. Maybe that was what gave her the idea for the ransom scheme. Or maybe they just helped her scheme along. Anyway, it seems to have worked, at least so far.

"Late last night your father's banker delivered half a million dollars to him. But after he went to sleep, someone broke into his room and stole the money."

Catarina buried her face in her hands. "My

poor father!" she moaned. "And he brought the money here for me! Because he loved me and wanted me with him!"

Nancy smiled gently. "I have a feeling that if we work fast, we'll be able to get that money back," she said. "Things are beginning to fall into place." She paused for a moment. "I can see how most of this was done," she said slowly, "and why. But there are a few things I just can't fit together."

"What?" Ned asked.

"That crazy spotted deer I saw," Nancy said. "And the kangaroo *you* saw, Gene. And the stock truck with no headlights."

"Stock truck?"

"Yes. Late last night I was nearly run down by a stock truck. It was running without lights, heading for the main road."

"But that doesn't make any sense," Gene protested. "We don't ship stock at night. If somebody brought any cattle in here, or took any out, I'd know about it in a minute."

"Smuggling!" Nancy exclaimed suddenly.

"What?" Gene demanded. "Smuggling? What are you talking about?"

"I think I know what's going on," Nancy exclaimed, snapping her fingers. "Even better, I think I know how to find out for sure. Come on, Gene! You're flying a bottle to San Antonio. And Ned and I are taking a horseback ride to explore a certain box canyon!"

Chapter

Sixteen

Nancy had taken Ned on a quick tour of the ranch and to meet Mr. Reigert, introducing him simply as a friend who had helped her on several other cases. Mr. Reigert, who was on his way to see the doctor in Rio Hondo, had only grunted a greeting. When Nancy had introduced Ned to Mrs. Reigert, she had been just as unfriendly.

When Nancy and Ned went out to the corral to saddle a couple of horses for their ride, they found Gene just climbing into the truck to leave for Rio Hondo. "It's noon now," he told Nancy. "I can be in San Antonio by two. The lab should be able to complete the tests in an hour. With luck, I ought to be back here by six—just before dinner."

Gene patted the bottle in his pocket. "I just hope the lab can tell us something definite," he said.

"Let's all meet in Mr. Reigert's office when you get back," Nancy suggested. "We've got to plan our strategy for the evening." She glanced at Ned. "I've already got some ideas, but we'll try to have something worked out by the time you get back."

Gene grinned at the two of them after he slammed the door of the pickup. "I bet you will," he said and drove off.

Instead of riding down through the lower canyon, as she had done earlier, Nancy and Ned guided their horses up the treacherous trail to the top of the limestone bluff. Nancy's palomino picked her way nervously through the rocks, staying away from the precipitous drop straight down to the right. Once or twice Nancy held her breath as large rocks, dislodged by the horses, tumbled down to the bottom of the cliff, several hundred feet below, but Ned rode confidently ahead.

It was nearly one-thirty by the time they reached the top of the bluff. They dropped their reins over the horses' ears to tether them while they made their way to the edge of the bluff to look over the box canyon.

Hidden from view in a clump of mesquite, Nancy knelt and put her binoculars to her eyes, peering into the canyon. She searched fruitlessly for a few minutes. There seemed to be nothing but willows and mesquite down there, growing around a small spring that opened into a muddy waterhole in the middle of the canyon. She could see a two-strand electric fence stretched across the front of the canyon. If anything was in there, it was penned in securely.

After a minute Ned touched her arm. "Look," he said, pointing toward the back of the canyon.

Then she saw what she was looking for. A herd of large brown deer, several with massive antlers —and *all* with white splotches! Most were lying peacefully in the high grass, while some stood under the willows, their mottled brown fur blending in beautifully with the dappled shade of the trees.

Nancy studied the deer for a few minutes and then swung her binoculars around the canyon, continuing her search. Suddenly, moving across the open grass, she saw a kangaroo! Impossibly, incredibly, unmistakably—a large brown kangaroo with muscular hind legs and a thick tail, moving through the tall grasses with short, powerful hops.

Nancy handed the binoculars to Ned and wiped the sweat out of her eyes. With those improbable deer and that out-of-place kangaroo down there, the canyon looked like a zoo. A refuge for exotic animals. At that moment Nancy remembered the conversation she had overheard between Mark and his "mother." Exotic animals! Smuggling!

"I've got it!" she exclaimed. "I know what Mark has been up to!"

"Yeah," Ned said. "It looks like he's got his own private exotic game reserve down there, doesn't it? I wouldn't be a bit surprised if those are endangered species."

"Right," Nancy said. "Probably so rare that he can't buy or sell them outright and has to smuggle them into the country."

"You know, that looks very much like a Sika deer to me," Ned replied, studying the herd of animals through the binoculars.

"Sika deer?"

"Sometimes you see them in zoos. They're extremely rare animals. I think they're from Formosa."

Nancy laughed a little. "It looks like Mark has found a way to go into the exotic game business, even without Mr. Reigert's permission."

After a little while Nancy and Ned climbed back on their horses and slowly returned to the ranch. Nancy was deep in thought. All of the pieces were definitely falling into place—but the only problem was proving what she knew.

There was nothing specific to link Mark to the exotic animals penned in the box canyon, and no proof that Mrs. Reigert was the one who had taken the money out of the safe the night before, or that she had sent the ransom notes. The attempts on Nancy's life could just as easily have been accidents. And so far, there was only Catarina's word that the bottle came from Mark's room.

Unless they could get confessions out of Mrs. Reigert and her "son," there didn't seem to be much chance that they would ever stand trial for their crimes.

Still, there might be a way. . . . Nancy smiled as a scheme began to form in her mind. It was a long shot, and it would require luck and careful planning, but it just might work.

"Hey, Ned," she said, riding up close to him. "What do you think about this?" And she told him her idea.

It was nearly three in the afternoon when Nancy and Ned got back to the ranch. They rode into the corral just as Mr. Reigert, looking tired and stooped, was returning from his trip to Rio Hondo to see the doctor. Ned took the horses to the stable to rub them down while Nancy followed Mr. Reigert to his room. He shut the door behind them and sat heavily on the edge of the bed.

"What did you learn?" Nancy asked. "Was the doctor able to tell you anything specific?"

Mr. Reigert shrugged. "Doctors are all alike," he muttered in disgust. "They take samples of all kinds and ask too many dumb questions. And then in the end they tell you that you'll just have to wait for the lab tests to come back."

Nancy's heart sank. She had hoped for some definite news before this evening. "Couldn't he even speculate?" she asked.

"Nope. But he *did* ask a bunch of questions about the funny garlic taste I've been getting," Mr. Reigert said, lying back wearily. "And he asked if I'd been losing any hair lately, or if I'd been short of breath."

"Losing hair?"

Mr. Reigert snorted. "Yeah. Crazy, isn't it? Of course I'm losing my hair, I told him. And I'm short of breath most of the time. That's what happens to people when they get to be my age."

"Did he say why he was asking these questions?"

"No," Mr. Reigert said shortly and closed his eyes. "Are you having any luck?"

"Yes, a little," Nancy said. Mr. Reigert's eyes flickered open. "But I don't want to talk about it just yet," she said hurriedly. If her plan was going to work, surprise was the most important part of it. She suspected that if Mr. Reigert knew about his daughter, he wouldn't be able to keep the secret very well. With a simple look or a gesture he could spoil everything.

"I'll let you know as soon as I find out anything definite," she promised. "By the way," she added, "my friend Ned would like to stay for supper. Would you have any objections?"

"Right now, I'm too tired to object to anything." Mr. Reigert sighed. "Guess I'm getting old. Do whatever you want to do. Invite anybody you want to invite." He opened one eye. "Except for Billy McPhee, of course. Now *git*. I need some sleep."

The rest of the afternoon seemed to crawl by. Nancy told Mrs. Reigert that there would be a guest for dinner. Mrs. Reigert didn't seem very pleased, but when Nancy said that Mr. Reigert had already given his permission, she nodded sullenly. Then Nancy and Ned sat under one of the large cottonwoods and talked over the events of the case while they waited for Gene to get back, bringing the lab report with him.

Finally, it was six o'clock, and the pickup pulled into the driveway. A few minutes later Ned and Nancy, Gene, Catarina, and Mrs. Arguello met in the office. Nancy locked the door and closed the blinds.

"What did you find out from the lab?" she asked Gene.

Gene put the little bottle on the desk. It was empty. "Poison, all right," he said. "The lab chief says it's called thallium sulfate. Some company up in Dallas used to sell it as an ant killer, but it was banned some years ago. Apparently, though, cans and bags of it are still being found in garages and barns where people have stored it and forgotten it."

He chuckled a little. "They took the stuff away from me. Guess they were afraid I might decide to use it on somebody."

Mrs. Arguello stared at the empty bottle. "I

think we used something like that years ago," she said. "To kill ants. The last time I saw it, it was in a can in the stable."

Gene looked troubled. "The chief also said that it would take only a gram of this stuff, administered cumulatively, to kill somebody."

Nancy glanced at him. "Do the symptoms of thallium poisoning include hair loss?" she asked. "The taste of garlic, shortness of breath?"

"How do you know all that?" Catarina asked in surprise as Gene nodded.

Ned grinned at Nancy. "Superior detective work," he replied. "Nancy Drew didn't get her reputation for nothing."

"Well, it looks like we've identified the poison," Nancy said. "Chances are that the would-be killer found this stuff here on the ranch somewhere, recognized it, and decided to use it. Our problem is to get the killer to confess to his crime." She looked around at the four intent faces. "Here's what I think we ought to do." They all leaned forward to listen to her plan.

It was nearly seven by the time everyone gathered around the dinner table. They were all there —Mr. Reigert, Mrs. Reigert and Mark, Gene, Joe Bob, Nancy and Ned. Nancy introduced Ned to Mark and Joe Bob, and they all sat down.

"Well, Nancy," Mark said heartily, passing her a plate heaped with corn bread, "what did you and your friend do today?"

"Not much," Nancy admitted, helping herself to one. "We went for a horseback ride, and then I spent the rest of the afternoon making notes on Mr. Reigert's project." It was all quite true, she thought to herself as she buttered her bread. Except that Mr. Reigert's "project" was very different from what Mark imagined.

"Well, I hope this thing isn't going to take much longer," Mrs. Reigert said pointedly. "I know you want to get it finished so that you can get on to other—"

She broke off her sentence and looked up sharply. Mrs. Arguello had come into the room and was leaning against the door, a wild-eyed expression on her face. "Mrs. Arguello, whatever are you doing?" she demanded. "We're waiting for the rest of our meal! What's keeping you?"

Mrs. Arguello looked around, her face ashen. *"Madre Dios,"* she whispered, her voice cracking. "It's the girl! In the library, on the floor. She's—she's—"

Nancy jumped up, knocking her chair over. She ran to Mrs. Arguello and shook her arm roughly. "What's happened?" she asked. "What are you trying to tell us?"

"Come on, woman," Mr. Reigert demanded impatiently. "You look like death itself! Spit it out! What's wrong?"

Suddenly Mrs. Arguello uttered a loud shriek, her eyes rolling back in her head. "It's the house-maid!" she cried. "She's dead!"

Chapter

Seventeen

Dead?" Mrs. Reigert screamed. "Oh, no!"

"But how?" Mr. Reigert asked, bewildered.

"Come on," Nancy commanded, and they all rushed into the library. On the floor, beside a large leather chair, lay the housemaid's crumpled body. At the sight of it, Mark's face went white. The girl's fingers were curled around the little bottle that she had taken from his room. But now the bottle was empty.

Nancy knelt beside the still form and felt for a pulse. After a moment she looked up. "Mrs. Arguello is right," she said soberly. "The girl is dead."

"But I just don't see how—" Mr. Reigert muttered. He sank into the leather chair. "It's unbelievable. She's so young!"

Nancy pulled out a handkerchief and carefully picked up the bottle. She opened the cap and sniffed it. "It's my guess that this is poison," she said. "In fact, it looks like it might be thallium sulfate, an ant poison commonly found in this part of the country."

She put the bottle down beside the body. "Gene, I think it's time to send for the sheriff."

"The sheriff?" Mark asked sharply. He licked his lips.

Gene made his way to the phone and began to dial. Mark took a step toward the body, his eyes on the bottle.

"Stay back," Nancy warned Mark while Gene asked to speak to the sheriff. "The body shouldn't be touched until the police arrive. They'll be especially interested in the fingerprints they find on that bottle." Then her eyes fell on something under Angela's hand and she picked it up. It was the silver button she had found under Mr. Reigert's window after the robbery.

Nancy looked up. "Mrs. Reigert," she said as if she were just remembering something, "didn't I see you wearing a shirt with buttons exactly like this on the day I arrived?"

Mrs. Reigert's mouth fell open and the blood drained from her face. "I—I—don't think—"

"Perhaps it would be a good idea if you would get that shirt and show us that it has all of its buttons," Nancy said.

"No!" Mrs. Reigert exclaimed. "I mean—" She turned to Mark. "Mark, what have you done?" she cried, her voice breaking. Her hands were clenched, her long fingernails digging into the palms of her hands. She was obviously on the verge of losing control. "Are you trying to—"

Suddenly she seemed to realize what she was saying, and she clamped her mouth shut and went rigid. "I don't know what you're talking about," she said to Nancy.

Nancy turned to Mark. His eyes were like dark wells in his face and he was breathing in great gulps. "Of course," she said carefully, watching Mark, "the first thing the police will do is take everyone's fingerprints. There are sure to be prints on the bottle. It will be a simple matter of matching them up."

Suddenly Mark broke. "I'm not going to let you frame me, Jonelle!" he shouted. He reached for her throat and pulled her in front of him, dragging a gun out from under his shirt. "You're the one who stole that bottle of ant poison out of my room, aren't you!" he screamed, holding her by the throat, her back to him. "You poisoned the girl just to frame me, so you could have all the money for yourself!"

Jonelle Reigert's fingers clutched at Mark's forearm as she tried to pull it from her throat.

"No!" she said, choking, her face red with exertion. "You're the one who's trying to frame *me*, putting my button under the body! You want them to think that *I'm* the one who did it! I don't know anything about any poison! I'd never have agreed to anything like *murder!*"

"Of course you knew about the poison," Mark growled menacingly into her ear, his grip tightening. It was as if the two of them, in their panic, had forgotten that the others were in the room. "Don't act so innocent! You couldn't possibly have thought that those stomach attacks were natural. You wanted the old man dead as much as I did."

Jonelle sagged against him, gasping for air. "Why would I?" she cried. "At least, not until I got my hands on the ransom money."

Mark put the gun behind Jonelle's ear. "What ransom money?" His eyes were narrow slits. "What are you talking about?"

"The half a million dollars that Jonelle took from the safe in Mr. Reigert's bedroom," Nancy said calmly, stepping forward. "You see, Mark, Jonelle was playing a clever little game, all for herself. She was taking Mr. Reigert for a fortune, and she didn't intend to let you have a penny."

"Half a million dollars?" Mark asked. His eyes darted in Nancy's direction.

"You know, it's a real shame, Mark," Nancy went on in a sympathetic voice. "Your plans might have worked out very nicely if Jonelle hadn't gotten greedy and decided to double-cross you."

147

"I didn't double-cross you, I swear it, Mark!" Jonelle cried, writhing in his tightening grasp. "I was planning to tell you about it, and as soon as the coast was clear we could—"

"You're lying," Mark said. His voice was steely. "I know you. You were out to take care of Number One. You don't care about anyone but yourself."

"Me? Well, what do you call that smuggling scheme you dreamed up without telling me? Why, that stupid little get-rich-quick trick nearly blew the whole thing! Kangaroos and spotted deer running around all over the place!"

"No, Jonelle," Nancy said. "It was your ransom scheme that blew everything. If it hadn't been for that, you and your friend Mark might have gotten out of this thing scot-free."

"Her *friend* Mark?" Mr. Reigert gasped, his eyes wide and staring.

"That's right, Mr. Reigert," Nancy said. "This pair of con artists aren't really mother and son." She gestured toward Ned. "Ned's found evidence that indicates what their backgrounds really are. And they aren't pretty, that's for sure."

With a great wrench, Jonelle finally managed to pull herself free of Mark's grasp. "It doesn't matter who we are or what we've done," she snarled. "You're not going to be able to press charges. Because if you do before we're far away, I'll have Catarina Reigert killed!" She turned to

Mr. Reigert, smiling cagily. "You see, Robert, I'm the only one who knows where your daughter is."

"No, Jonelle," Nancy corrected her gently. "You *don't* know. In fact, I think you're going to be rather surprised when you learn just where Catarina is."

"What are you talking about?" Jonelle demanded. She's being held in Dallas. By some friends of mine. And if you don't let us go, she'll be killed." She turned triumphantly to Mr. Reigert. "Your precious daughter—dead! How would you like that?"

Mr. Reigert moaned. "We can't do anything, Nancy," he whispered, dropping his head into his hands. "I want my daughter back! I don't care what it costs!"

"You'll have her, Mr. Reigert," Nancy promised. She turned to the figure lying on the floor. "It's time, Catarina," she said. "You can get up now."

And with a smile on her face, Catarina got to her feet and ran to Mr. Reigert. "Here I am, Father," she whispered, pulling his hands away from his face.

"Angela? Catarina?" Mr. Reigert gasped, bewildered. "Is it true? Is it really true?"

"Show him, Catarina," Nancy commanded.

Catarina lifted her ankle, pulling back her skirt. "The birthmark, Father," she said proudly.

For a moment Mr. Reigert stared at her. And then he pulled her down into the chair with him, enveloping her in an enormous embrace. "Catarina," he murmured into her hair. "My child! It is really you, after all these years!"

"Oh, no," Jonelle Reigert groaned tearfully. "I don't believe it!"

"Well, you're not going to stop me from getting away," Mark screamed. "I've still got all the aces." He brandished the gun. "Okay, everybody line up against that wall, hands over your— oomph!" In an instant the gun had gone flying, Mark had been pushed into Jonelle, and Ned was standing coolly over both of them.

"That's the end of *that*," he said, dusting his hands.

"Maybe," Nancy said, smiling at Mr. Reigert and his daughter, still holding each other. "But wouldn't you say that it's just the beginning of something else?"

"I don't understand how I could have been so stupid," Mr. Reigert said. "How could I have been taken in so thoroughly?"

They were sitting around the kitchen table, having a quiet cup of coffee after Billy McPhee had come and carted Mark and Jonelle off to the Rio Hondo jail for safekeeping. Apparently the sheriff was skilled at collecting criminals and taking confessions, even though he might not have been much good at apprehending them or figuring out what they were up to.

"They're pretty slick characters," Nancy said. "And you're obviously not the first person they've taken."

"Right," Ned observed from his seat next to Nancy. "The police know of at least one person they've conned in Dallas. I assume there are many more."

"Have we tied up all the other loose ends?" Gene asked, holding up his cup so that Mrs. Arguello could pour him another cup of coffee. He leaned back in his chair and put his arm around Catarina's shoulders as she smiled happily at him.

Nancy began to tick the items off on her fingers. "As far as the phony kidnapping was concerned, it looks as if Jonelle was responsible for that all alone," she said.

"She planned to make off with the ransom money and leave Mark in the lurch. From what she said before the sheriff came to pick her up, I gather that she must have gotten the idea for the fake kidnapping when she came across the clothing stored in the attic. Then she sent the ransom notes and hired someone to impersonate Catarina on the videotape.

"The night of the robbery, she looked out her window and saw Mr. Lawson and me and concluded that he was bringing the money. It was an easy matter to unlock the safe, using the combination she had copied out of Mr. Reigert's drawer. But now the money's back in Mr. Reigert's safe.

"Mark was solely responsible for the smuggling scheme and the poisoning," Mr. Reigert said thoughtfully. "Apparently, my wife didn't know anything about that part of it." He grimaced as he said the word *wife*.

"Yes," Nancy agreed. After Ned had knocked Mark down, he had fallen apart, confessing everything, confirming what she and Ned already suspected about the smuggling operation. "The animals we saw in the canyon represented just one shipment, a half dozen extremely rare Sika deer from Formosa. There had been several other shipments of rare or endangered species, all smuggled in from Asia."

Ned turned his coffee cup in his hand. "They were trucking the animals across the Rio Grande from Mexico," he said, "pasturing them in that canyon until buyers were found. Then they trucked them out again. Apparently, it was quite a lucrative business."

"You know, Gene," Mr. Reigert said thoughtfully, "it might not be such a bad idea to look into the exotic game business—legally, of course," he added hastily.

Gene laughed. "That's just what I was thinking," he said.

Mr. Reigert turned to Nancy. "And what about

the poison?" he asked. He frowned. "I'm not going to die, am I—at least, not from that stuff?"

"According to the report that Gene brought back from the lab in San Antonio, it turns out to be a case of thallium poisoning," Nancy said. "Mark must have found the tin that was stored in the stables, recognizing its potential, and begun to use it very judiciously, knowing that it's a cumulative poison. Of course, he figured that nobody would suspect anything when you died, since the poisoning would look like a chronic stomach condition. And he and Jonelle could easily ensure that there wouldn't be an autopsy."

Mr. Reigert shuddered. "I hate to think what would have happened if you hadn't figured it all out, Nancy."

Nancy grinned. "It doesn't look like you've suffered any permanent damage," she said. "But it might not be a bad idea to go back to that doctor in Rio Hondo for another checkup."

"Not on your life!" Mr. Reigert said, banging his fist on the table. "Now that this is over, you won't catch me *dead* in that doctor's office!"

"Now, Father," Catarina said softly. She got up and stood behind him, putting her arms around his neck. "Won't you be reasonable about this? Just for me?"

Mr. Reigert's face softened. "Well," he said grumpily, "I'll think about it." He looked at Nancy. "Nancy Drew, I don't know how I can ever thank you," he said. "My daughter and I are back together, and it looks as if I'm going to get a fine son-in-law in the bargain. What can I do to repay you?"

Nancy stood up and stretched. "I'll just settle for a walk through the garden—with Ned," she said, smiling at him.

Ned stood up and put his arm around her shoulders. "I can't think of a better ending."

Nancy's next case:

Poor little rich boy Hal Colson has been kidnapped
—and his guardian wants Nancy to deliver the ransom. Nancy always thought that guardians were
stuffy and old. But Lance Colson is handsome and
young.

Then the plan goes disastrously wrong. The kidnappers think Nancy has cheated them out of their
money! Nancy must find Hal Colson before this
ransom scheme gets him killed.

Can Nancy beat the kidnappers? Find out in *FATAL
RANSOM*, Case #12 in The Nancy Drew Files™.